For a helpless, primitive planet, Jsimaj was doing all right for itself.

In the first place, Belaker Meas had been captured, almost immediately and in no uncertain manner, by a bunch of drovers herding the twelve-legged multipedes native to the planet.

The drovers were clearly a resourceful and courageous lot, but the rendals were about as twitchy as anything that big could get, not to say downright panicky.

Furthermore, Meas shrewdly suspected that the drovers believed his story of being a religious figure of some kind as much as he did. They were understandably suspicious of his constant need to go off and "pray"—rightly so, for actually he was reporting to his partner in orbit around Jsimaj. Not that being in communication was meant to do Meas any good—it was simply that in the likely event of his being killed, CROWN would not have made their heavy investment for nothing. And that was just the beginning . . .

A WORLD OF TROUBLE

Robert E. Toomey, Jr.

BALLANTINE BOOKS—NEW YORK

Copyright © 1973 by Robert E. Toomey, Jr.

All rights reserved.

SBN 345-03262-4-125

First Printing: May, 1973

Printed in the United States of America

Cover art by Dean Ellis

BALLANTINE BOOKS, INC.
101 Fifth Avenue, New York, N.Y. 10003

DEDICATION

To Lee Hoffman
With love,
For opening doors,
And without whom,
Et cetera.

Many people used to believe that angels moved the stars. It now appears that they do not. As a result of this and like revelations, many people do not now believe in angels.

—R. D. Laing

Part One: The Arrival

We translated into =relativistic= space, and my spirit warily rejoined my flesh. I felt wrung out, used up, done in. Neostasis does that to you. My head was full of the things I didn't like to think about. I swung my feet over the side of the rack and set up. Sensation slowly, and not too gracefully, returned to me.

Pacesetter was wailing in his makeshift stall. His claws rang against the metal deck. I mumbled something to him so he'd know that I understood. He ignored me completely. To regain your lost perspective, you have to externalize. You have to find a way to occupy your attention.

I began to tie knots in my holy blue cord. Each knot went right over left, right over left, left over right, up, under, through, around twice, loop, reverse, then repeat. It's an intricate knot, and it has to be done just so, or start it again. My fingers were clumsy with the cord. I worked at it very carefully.

On the other side of the cabin, the pilot disconnected himself from his stat rig, and plugged in the master control panel. His name was Peter Donovan, a thirteen year old genius. He'd been trained nearly from birth in a variety of esoterica, but none of his training had included good manners. His attitude constantly rubbed me the wrong way.

He looked like a poster boy for CROWN's pilot recruiting program. His hair was a rusty reddish brown that fell cunningly into his eyes, which were a bright inquisitive blue. Across the bridge of his nose was a spray of freckles, guaranteed to gladden the hearts of grandmothers everywhere. He wore a standard singlepiece olive drab uniform, with an ornate coronet stitched on over the pocket in silver thread.

He spoke to me and I glanced up. The cabin lights were dim. The lights from the control panel were a sweet confusion of melting colors. As I watched, an ice blue blinked aquamarine, then dissolved to amber. A pale green glowed, not dissimilar to the shade of Pacesetter's hide. It came and went in an instant, replaced by deep indigo.

"Say again," I said.

"That thing." He pointed at the stall. "Your pet."

"What about him?"

"He's a noisy pain in the ass."

"Softly Peter." I finished a knot and began another. "You'll hurt his feelings."

"This is a personnel spacecraft," Peter said sharply, "not a cattle carrier. It was designed to very precise specifications to hold a maximum of three *human beings* in relative comfort. Not two human beings and a caterpillar legged monster that howls like a demented banshee six hours out of every nine."

"He's just not used to space travel." I gestured with the cord. "For that matter, neither am I."

"But you're not so fucking vocal about it," Peter said. "And I don't care much for the way he chomps his fangs. He makes me feel as if I'm part of the menu."

"Pacesetter's a sworn vegetarian and a lot less likely to have you for dinner than you are to have him."

Peter grunted rudely. "I'd eat dirty underwear first."

"Would you now?"

"Without salt," he said.

He returned to his instruments. I got up and went over to the stall, and put my arm in the multipede's mouth. He calmed down at once and stared at me with idiot love in his glassy green eyes. I stared back at him and cooed about how brave and beautiful I thought he was. He snuffled in reply.

Multipedes are as affectionate as puppy dogs, though a bit more unwieldy, and loyal to a fault when you show them you care. But it's no use scratching them behind the ears, or where their ears would be if they had any. Not unless you do it with a pickaxe. They don't feel much through all that armor plating.

"Peter," I said.

"What?"

"There are lots of things that are worse than having a multipede on your hands."

He turned from his nest of color with an unconvinced expression on his face. "Name one."

"Did you ever hear of a planet called Bloomer?"

He shook his head. "It's not a regularly scheduled stop."

"That's right," I said. "A while ago, I had a job there, strip mining." Actually it was more like a prison sentence, but that was none of his business. "And Bloomer had a problem."

"The atmosphere?"

"Nope."

"The weather?"

"Nope."

"The natives?"

"Nope."

"I give up."

"The guano."

He frowned. "The—guano?"

"Yeah," I said. "The vulgar call it birdshit. It makes an excellent organic fertilizer."

"You mean you were mining the planet for *birdshit*?" he asked, interested in spite of himself.

I winked at Pacesetter. "Not quite. I was mining the planet for radioactives. Old Bloomer had almost as high a radioactives supply as Jsimaj here. My job was keeping track of the automatic digging machinery. All I was supposed to do was watch the dials and needles and little flashes on the comp board."

"Soft," Peter said.

"You think so?"

"Wasn't it?"

"Hardly," I said. "Guano defeated the machinery. It kept on seeping into the gear housings where the watertight seams had pulled apart under the stress of running eighteen hours a day at one point four gees. The guano was like a combination of paste and putty, a glorious stinking mess, great for gardens and farms, for plastering cracks in the wall, or for mailing to conservative politicians C.O.D. You could also model with it if you got your kicks that way."

"So you had to keep cleaning shit off the machines," Peter said. "I certainly hope you had a decent pair of gloves."

"You haven't got the idea yet," I said. "The machinery had to be broken down, and the guano, which hardened at approximately the speed of light, had to be loosened with corrosive acid, then chipped away at with hammer and chisel. Chipped very carefully so as not to bruise any of the delicate gears, since the nearest replacement center was a week and a half away. Then the seams had to be rewelded, and the process began all over again."

Peter wrinkled his nose. "What a drag."

"I did it for six months."

"Six months." His voice skidded upwards into a pubescent squeal that made Pacesetter blink. "How the hell did you manage to stick it out so long?"

"Unwavering resolve," I said. "But there's more to the story. Besides the guano, which was bad, I was completely alone, which was terrible. And not only that, the local flora and fauna were inedible, so I had to bring my own stuff. I had one hundred and fifty crates of synthayeast in twelve delicious flavors."

"Yucch," Peter said.

"You've tried it."

"Just once."

"Once is enough," I said. "Steak loses something after it's gone through a Morgenson Blender and come out mucilage, no matter how dietetically nutritional it is for you and your family. So you must agree that there really are worse things than having a multipede on your hands in a three man spaceship cabin." I stared at him keenly to see if the moral had penetrated.

He appeared to consider it for a moment, and then he said in a final tone, "There are better things too."

He returned to his instruments again. I took my arm out of Pacesetter's mouth. Love is not won without cost. The sleeve of my tunic was soaked with it. I wacked the multipede on the snout to let him know that everything was fine between us, and then I went back to my rack to sit down and tie some more knots. Shortly I fell asleep and dreamed of endless bomb runs of guano.

I awakened with Peter shaking me.

"Don't look up," I shouted.

"Why would I want to do that?" he said. "Our ETA's about twenty minutes from now."

I yawned. "Okay."

"Good."

I sat up and rubbed the sleep out of my eyes. Peter went back to his station. I was still tired, but the nap had done wonders, had cheered me. Even Pacesetter seemed more relaxed and happy. At least he was quieter. Maybe he knew he was almost home. I envied him that knowledge if he had it. Not everyone has a home to return to.

I could see Jsimaj on the viewscreen above Peter's head. It was just a circle in silhouette. Here on the night side, the sun was hidden from us. And we were hidden from the sun. Our course would take us straight to a part of the world where the night was deepest. We were sneaking in so as not to attract any undue attention. With luck we might not attract any due attention either.

The nap must have improved my manual dexterity too. I did up my last few knots with little trouble. Then I shucked my tunic, and dressed myself in the desert robes of a kirlu, a sort of itinerant holy man. Under the robes I wore nothing but a thin loincloth to help prevent chafing and rash. When I got to the desert the robes would be rather warm, but they would also afford me protection from sun and sand. I was going to need that protection.

The robes were cinctured at the waist with my blue cord, tied now with the seven complex knots that bound the seven spirits of the day. I added seven tiny brazen bells to the cord to amuse the seven ghouls of the evening. My sandals of multipede hide completed the outfit. I'd been wearing them for weeks, except when I wore no shoes at all, to properly batter my feet. A simple lack of ingrained grime and callouses could arouse enough suspicion to blow my entire disguise. And that could be fatal.

My name is Belaker Meas, rhymes with keys. I'm economically built, with dark brown eyes, and dark brown skin. When I was a boy my mother used to tell me out ancestors were tribal chieftains. Depending on the mood I'm in, I sometimes like to repeat the tale, though it probably isn't true. Irishmen claim descent from a race of barbarian kings. Congolese claim descent from tribal chieftains. It's fortunate for the rest of you that both the groups are becoming extinct, are being absorbed into the main mass of untitled humanity. Otherwise you'd never hear the end of it.

"Deceleration in one minute," Peter said without looking up from what he was doing.

I nodded. "Right."

"The correct response is roger."

"Too formal," I said.

He was firm. "The correct response is roger."

"Come off it."

"The correct—"

I clenched my fists. "So roger already."

"Right," he said.

I strapped into my rack with my bells going jingle tinkle jingle. Pacesetter would have to fend for himself from here to the ground, but I wasn't much concerned about his welfare. He had twelve sturdy legs to support him. Of course there was always the off chance that he might break one. But his weight, somewhere in the neighborhood of a thousand kilos, was pretty evenly distributed. And if he did happen to break a leg he could still manage fine on the remaining eleven until it healed or regenerated.

"Deceleration in thirty seconds," Peter said.

"Roger."

"Excellent."

"Thank you," I said.

A pause.

"Deceleration in ten seconds."

"Roger."

"Nine seconds."

"Roger."

"Eight seconds."

"Roger."

"You can stop saying roger."

"Roger."

The rockets cut in with a throbbing roar, the transition as smooth as silk. Peter knew his business, I had to admit it. The pressure gradually increased as we traded the artificial gravity producing residual spin for a stabilizing thrust. And like a giant compass needle turning slowly towards a distant magnetic north, the *Shoten Zenjin* pointed its polished steel nose at the hot black midsection of the planet below.

I kept my eyes on the viewscreen.

       Night.

Closer and closer, blacker and blacker.

The viewscreen picture altered to an infrared reading as we made our approach.

Directly below us was the continent of Eltovi. Running most of the way across it, like a maimed and twisted spinal column, were the Mountains of Edujan, subdividing the continent into two unequal parts. The mountains were named after a local deity, the god of chance and odd circumstances.

Eltovi was shaped roughly like a lopsided shark, with an outsize offcenter dorsal fin. The fin was the peninsula Klask, and at its base, near the mountains, was the major city of Klask'an. Curving around the city was the River of Peace. It flowed out of a large natural cavern that went all the way through Edujan and emptied into the sea.

The river was misnamed if my information on it was accurate. Its waters had, at various times in the history of Jsimaj, run a cloudy red, and its deltas had been clogged with human sediment. War here was still a bloody clash, fought with naked blades and muscle. They hadn't cleaned it up yet, and given it over to the button pushers. What a shame, what a mess. But progress would square them away.

One side of Edujan was mainly desert. Except for the

immediate area around Klask'an, there was only one other sizable settlement. This community had developed some distance away in a sprawling oasis, where a bottomless lake sustained several multipede ranches, and a collection of farmers and tradesmen. There were other oases in the desert, but all of them were small, and none were fertile enough to support many permanent residents.

The further side of Edujan had more character. There was a disreputable forest situated in a pocket of high radioactivity, vast stretches of marshy swampland, and some very scenic country with decent soil and a slightly cooler climate. The people here were spread out, living in villages and towns, and they rarely got into trouble. Wars were uncommon among them.

The rest of the planet was of no further interest. It was for the most part untenanted. The radioactives were the prize. So high was the count in some places on Eltori that mutations were produced. Pacesetter was one of these. His species began with a sport that had proven viable and bred true. Now multipedes were the main source of transportation on Jsimaj.

Sometime earlier CROWN had sent a survey team in to check the planet out. They mapped it and learned local customs and languages. When they left, a contact man remained behind to send back reports on what was happening there, if anything. The contact man's name was Jules Atherton. His reports had come through regularly and on schedule. And then they had suddenly stopped. I was here to find out why.

The pressure increased to a point where I wasn't able to watch the viewscreen anymore. My eyes crossed and I had to close them. When I opened them again we'd landed, and Peter was swinging in his seat, kicking out his legs. He stood up and waved his arms around windmill fashion.

"I can hear the bones crackle," he said.

I unstrapped myself. "My bones have disintegrated." Pacesetter was rearing in his stall. "Get down," I told him. "You can play all you want outside."

"Stupid brute." Peter scowled at the multipede.

"What's the scene out there?" I asked.

"Sparse vegetation," he said, "most of it stumpy. Lots of sand. Some minor animal life I can't identify for you. And about twenty kilometers from here, between us and the city, there's a gathering of multipedes and people."

"A big gathering?"

He shrugged idly. "Depends on what you consider big."

"I consider big my desire to know how many of them there are," I said. "Try naming something specific for me, like a number for instance."

"The best I can give you is an estimate."

"Give me an estimate."

"Less than a thousand." He began doing setups. "Maybe less than half that, with more multipedes than people."

Exercise seemed like a good idea, so I cracked my knuckles. "If it's a herd, there's drovers driving them. That means I might not have to go into Klask'an alone. They might serve as a screen for my arrival."

"They might also be bandits."

"In which case, I bite my tooth."

"That would certainly screw up the plan," Peter said.

I didn't reply to him. Inside my false upper teeth were a series of compartments containing a limited but neat pharmacopoeia of drugs. I had a truth serum, an anesthetic, an antibiotic, and a stimulant. And a quick relief poison for use while being tortured or otherwise harshly dealt with. The bandits here were savage, and my venom was painless. Behind my left ear was a powerful surgically implanted supersubmicrominiaturized radio pickup that sent sound straight to the brain. In my throat was a tiny transmitter. These were my tenuous links with the ship. But for them and my drug store, I wasn't carrying any technical apparatus, and I wasn't supposed to be needing any.

Peter would maintain the *Shoten Zenjin* in a parking orbit above Jsimaj and monitor my signal. But he wouldn't be of much help if things really started to get rough. It was strictly against the rules for him to show himself to the native population. That would constitute direct interference with a primitive culture. CROWN would be heavily censured in the Great and General Council of Worlds for it, and this would tend to reflect no glory on CROWN's benevolent public stance of neutrality and nonaggression. So basically I was on my own.

I put my arm in Pacesetter's mouth to keep him calm and unlatched his stall gate. Peter finished up his deep knee bends, then pressed the proper stud on the control panel, and the airlock cycled open. I had not the vaguest notion which stud it was, and if Peter had died for some reason during transit, I would have been in real trouble. I couldn't have gone to the toilet by myself, let alone figure out the workings of the ship. Pilots have a terrific secrecy fetish, almost as bad as governments have. They won't tell you nothing about nothing, unless it's something you don't want to hear.

"Come on Pacesetter," I said.

Peter grinned. "Goodbye brute."

Pacesetter gave out with a screech of pure joy and bounded—try to imagine him bounding in that compact cabin, it's a wonder my arm didn't bound right along with him—bounded over to the dc chamber. The access ramp slid out and down with a whirr of smoothly functioning machinery. Pacesetter, bless his hearts, dashed down it ecstatically, and into the desert night.

"Don't wander too far," I called after him, following at a more subdued pace.

HEAT

"Wow," Peter said, at my heels.

"Jesus!" I agreed.

This place was the maw of a blast furnace. I broke out at once in a clammy sweat. By the light from the cabin behind him, I could see a sheen of perspiration glazing Peter too. He wiped his face on a sleeve.

"The days here must be awful," he said.

"Clear and warmer according to the official forecast." I leaned into the slant of the ramp for balance.

He touched my shoulder briefly. "You'll roast alive."

"I'm roasting already," I said.

"So am I."

"But you don't have to get used to it."

"True," he said.

"Then go back in the ship where it's cool."

"In a minute."

I stared at the starry sky. "No sign of rain."

"Not much sign of anything," he said.

We had reached the desert floor. To the left, Edujan gloomed over us, dark and sheer, with ragged unclimbable cliffs. To the right, and ahead and below, was a vista of sand, appearing oddly glacial by the moonlight. We stood there in it and we sweltered, me especially in my holy robes.

An infinitude of stars twinkled through the black. They were nearly worth the trip in themselves. Night is always beautiful when you see it, though it looks about the same most anywhere. It just seems there's so much more of it in some places than there is in others.

"It's quiet here, isn't it?" Peter said softly. "After the ship, I mean."

"Listen," I said.

In the distance something howled, a mournful solitary keening, across the great emptiness. Something answered, equally mournful. A wind arose. My bells jingled. The seven ghouls of the evening were presumably amused. And Pacesetter was glad to be home again. He was gazing in the sparse desert shrubbery as though his life depended on it.

And Tarbah the moon was glad. Soon she would join Tarban, her spouse, out of sight now. Together they would make the celestial love that had given birth to Jsimaj, and incidentally to the rest of the universe that surrounded it. The moon was just as beat up and pitted with meteor craters as any other moon. A little more silvery and bright perhaps.

I felt a rush of something, maybe a sense of vastness, maybe something else. I glanced at Peter. He was gazing off in no particular direction. The shadow of the ship fell across us, a stark arrow pointing towards my next stop. The thought came to me that they were all next stops. There were no destinations in sight. Not for me there weren't. There hadn't been for some time now.

Pacesetter came over, and nudged me with his snout, very gently, snorting in basso profundo. It meant that he was feeling insecure and wanted reassurance. I reassured him. He drifted away to a patch of intensified darkness that was probably something only he could find edible. He began to munch on it. The noise he made was like that of gravel being pulverized under a millstone.

A multipede looks like a three way evolutionary draw between an armadillo and a dachshund and approximately two clydesdales. Built low to the ground, they're pale green and all armor, except for the speckled white belly. A full grown one is as high as a man's chest and as long as a boring afternoon. Down the neck is a cartilaginous crest, exactly right for hanging onto. You throw a blanket on the back of one and you're off. Sometimes with a crash.

Just walking around he looks like a joke, constructed entirely of leftover parts. But when he starts to run you suddenly see the method underlying the merriment. He gathers himself up and he runs. And he runs fast. And he runs tirelessly, for hours on end. You notice the streamlining then, and wonder why you missed it before. All those legs going at once, in a pale green blur. And one hundred and ten kph. Quite a sport.

You don't learn to ride one like you learn to drive a hovercopt. At first you sort of cautiously clamber aboard and hold on for dear life while he takes it slow and easy. Then you gain courage. The speed goes up a notch. You gain more courage. The speed goes up more notches. You have it down. Then you're zooming along like the devil in a soul sprint, and you're feeling that wonderful bracing wind of passage.

Only sometimes it isn't bracing enough. You remember that even forty or fifty kph is still damn fast, particularly if that's the rate at which you're plowing up the ground with your sternum. It can be a harrowing experience. Fortunately the broken ribs heal swiftly with modern medical techniques. And finally you know how to do the thing, and you realize that it's almost fun. At the very least you get a sense of accomplishment from it.

"Peter," I said.

"Hummph."

"Toss some sand at me."

He was puzzled. "What?"

"Sand," I said. "It's this here granular stuff underfoot here." I picked up a handful to illustrate. "See?"

"I know what sand is." He squatted irritably and let it sift through his fingers. "Why toss it at you?"

"Verisimilitude," I said. "I wish to appear the traveler. Our friends up ahead would expect certain things of such a person. One of these things is a coating of trail dust."

"Tricky," he said.

"I try."

We commenced an intramural sand tossing festival. Peter tossed it at me. I called Pacesetter over and tossed it at him. The wind that had come up earlier intensified, and shortly we were all hip deep in the grit. Peter gestured at me.

"Enough?"

I glanced down at myself. "More than enough. Now why don't you go back inside the ship and check out our radio equipment?"

"Okay."

"The correct response is roger."

"Up yours," he said.

He brushed ineffectually at his uniform as he mounted the ramp. The sand was mildly adhesive. He'd have to change his clothes to get rid of it. But Pacesetter shed it from his scales without any effort, and went off hunting for another juicy clump of vegetation. Sand was his element. It didn't bother him a bit.

EEEEEEEEEEEEEE

Feedback ripped through my headset.

"Turn down the fucking volume," I screamed, clapping both hands to my ears, as though it would do any good.

"*Sorry Meas*," came a far away voice that stabbed at my aching forebrain. "*How's this?*"

"Much better." I pushed my eyes back into their sockets, where they resettled themselves with some reluctance, staring offward in opposite directions. "Raise the volume, just a trifle."

"*Like this?*"

"A trifle more."

"*Is this it?*"

"More."

"*Am I there yet?*"

"You're there, freeze it." My forebrain twinged with each word. "How am I coming through?"

"*Five by five.*"

"Fantastic," I said. "Come on back out here. Bring me my water bag and the blanket it's wrapped in. I forgot them before."

"*Where are they?*"

"In the cabinet labeled Truth and Beauty under my rack."

"*Okay,*" he said soberly.

His transmitter clicked off. The pain in my skull had receded to a numbing tenor buzz in the frontal lobes, and I was beginning to feel as though I might survive the initial impact. I chased up Pacesetter and held him steady. Peter arrived and gave me the bag and the blanket.

"Take care," he said.

"I will."

He turned and headed back to the ship again. I drank some water. Pacesetter drank somewhat more. Then I laid the blanket across him, got aboard, took up the reins, thumped his auditory surface, and we were off. Peter paused at the top of the ramp, the lighted airlock like a bright halo around him. Saint Peter, a laugh. I watched him watch me go, until we couldn't see each other any more.

If you've never ridden a multipede, and chances are good that you haven't, it's hard to describe the sensation. Pacesetter was moving along at a nonchalant lope, no faster than twenty or thirty kph. The motion wasn't up and down as it would have been on a horse. Not with twelve legs going in synchronized order. But he did sway from side to side as he ambled along.

Actually this made for a fairly smooth ride. The only problem is that, as the multipede sways from side to side, so does the rider. You go forty degrees to the right, and then back in the direction of his rump. Then you go forty degrees to the left. You lean forward, hanging onto the reins, and grip the rigid crest. Then you repeat the whole act. You are going in a circle.

This can make you quite dizzy, and it's the major thing you have to get used to, after you learn how to stay on. Getting used to it, back on Earth, I went through six phials of cyclizine hydrochloride, twelve to a phial, in the first six days. After that I began to improve by small increments, and by now I had it all totally under control. Of course I still barfed occasionally, but that didn't mean a thing.

Behind us, the *Shoten Zenjin* thundered, spilled out flame, and hurtled upwards.

Goodbye Peter.

I was on my own.

The heat was intense. I was sweating vigorously. The dust caked to mud on me and stuck to my flesh. It absorbed my bodily fluids, gained weight from them, and hung on me like malignant tumors. The wind continued to blow, though less than before. My cowl went a long way towards guarding my face, but it was filling up fast with sand. I partially solved that by pinching it shut over my nose, and gripping the rigid crest tighter with the other hand. Breathing wasn't exactly easy, but at least it was possible.

For Pacesetter the desert was no trouble at all. He was nicely adapted to his environment, with scales that shed the sand, and nictitating lids that protected his eyes. I could have used some of that protection myself. Even with my eyes slitted down to near blindness, the sand would gather on lash and rim, then sneak in underneath, where it hurt. Finally I gave up and closed my eyes completely, leaving the tears to cleanse them as best they could. And it was sway to the right, then back, and sway to the left, then forward, around in a circle around. Exhaustion from neostasis was catching up with me. I let go of the reins.

I was falling a—

sleep.

A change in the rhythm of Pacesetter's stride caused me to open my eyes a bit. The wind had slackened even more. Through slits I could see a campfire flickering up ahead and many moving shapes. The mountains were still to my left. The campfire was jammed into a cliff outcropping that would box out the worst of a crosswind. A lot of multipedes were lowing and, as we approached at a slow trot, I heard a loud cry from above.

I glanced up and saw a figure coming down at me from a shelf of rock. I had no time to react. His swirling clothes turned his shadow into that of a huge predatory night bird. Then he hit me. I was bowled off Pacesetter's back and slammed to the ground. The multipede went one way and my breath went the other.

The figure regained his feet at once, and the prow of his sword pinned me to the sand by the neck. I was afraid to swallow, for fear my adam's apple would catch on the sharp edge, which was flush against my throat. By the light of the moon I could see the man's face. He looked very unfriendly.

Irrelevant thoughts go through your mind at times like that. Someone brought a torch and it occurred to me to wonder where the wood for it and the campfire had come from out in the middle of this treeless waste. I was pleased when the answer came to me. Some of the multipedes were undoubtedly being used as pack animals, hauling all the necessary supplies of food and timber.

"Are you a demon?" the man with the sword asked me in the tone of a prosecuting attorney.

"A demon?" I couldn't imagine where he could have gotten such a weird idea.

"Have you come to tempt and destroy us?"

"No," I said. "No."

"Do you deny that you're a demon?"

"I deny it."

"You're a liar," he said. "Demons always lie."

His bearded features were mean and black and angry, and his hulk of a body was set in a posture of retribution. I squirmed my head and shoulders deeper into the sand to get some distance on his blade. He kept it flush to my throat. I stopped squirming. It was essential for me to act like the sort of person I was supposed to be. I took a breath and projected as much unruffled pious dignity as I could manage from a supine position.

"This is nonsense," I said. "I am Gnarla, a simple kirlu. Ytrifg The Inscrutable is my illustrious lord."

"Liar," said the swordsman, his blade moving slightly.

My skin puckered up around it, as though to kiss away my life. "I am not a demon." Hey there, skin, I thought, unpucker.

"But we saw your star fall from the sky," he said conclusively, "and then we saw it return to the sky." So that was where he got such a weird idea.

"And you rode out of the darkness from the same direction as that star," said the torchbearer. "Is it possible for this to be a coincidence?"

"Nothing more," I said with the utter conviction of falsehood. "A coincidence and nothing more."

"Clarowdung," said the swordsman, meaning multipede shit, the local term for it.

"Draw your blade back a little," I said, "and I will show you your mistake."

The swordsman turned to the torchbearer. "He's a demon."

"Perhaps."

"We should quarter him."

"Not so hastily," I said hastily. "Consider your decision. Draw back your blade. Let me prove myself to you."

"It can't hurt to do what he asks," the torchbearer said, stepping closer. "We can split him in a while if he warrants it."

The swordsman shrugged, and said to me, "An unwise move will bring your demon lies to an abrupt end." His blade drew back, but not very far.

"I will raise my hand," I said. "I beg you not to read menace into the motion."

"Go on," said the torchbearer.

"Slowly," said the swordsman.

A crowd had gathered, men and women and kids. They were all quite silent, and I couldn't see their expressions in the dimness. That was probably just as well. I brought up my hand and tested the chevron point of the blade. It was sharp enough to do the job. I gritted my teeth and made a shallow slash across the ball of my thumb. The blood came out like ink in the torchlight.

"I am but a mortal man," I said, "no different from any of you." I brandished my bloody thumb. "This proves it."

A murmur went through the crowd.

"Lies and illusions," the swordsman said. "It is well known that a demon once stole human form and dwelt for nineteen matings of the moons in a cave by the ancient village of Dwarn'ir. There he misled all passersby until he was slain by a man of stout spirit. Hirag, was it not?" He appealed to the crowd for confirmation.

"Hirag slew the demon of Ogleefra, who took the likeness of a monster fion," someone said at the edge of the group.

"That was Horin," said the swordsman. "You have them confused. Horin slew the demon fion of Ogleefra."

"He slew a monster tagel," said another in the crowd.

"You're thinking of Megis," said the swordsman. "He slew a demon tagel at Fruhs. It was devouring all the village children."

"And all the village virgins too," someone added.

"The girls were pleading with the boys to save them," someone else said. "I only wish I'd been there. I'd have saved every one of them."

"First you'd have to have saved yourself," yelled a woman from the rear.

"I wouldn't have saved you to do it," he said.

The discussion then began to deteriorate. Meanwhile the blood that was running out of my thumb and over my wrist and down my arm was congealing. I lay on the hot sandy ground and I sweated. The people in the crowd argued back and forth about this and that. My stomach rumbled. I was getting hungry.

The swordsman called for attention. It was easy to see that he enjoyed these myths a lot, and that he liked to identify with their protagonists. And here I was, his ticket into folklore. All he had to do was kill me, assuming that I was a demon. But at the moment he was trying to shut everyone up.

"Be quiet," he said.

"Die in bed," someone told him.

He peered at the crowd. "Name yourself and we'll see which of us dies where."

"I take it back," the someone said.

The swordsman nodded, flexed his muscles, put a foot on my chest, and then said, "Horin slew the demon flon of Ogleefra. Megis slew the demon tagel at Fruhs. Hirag was the hero of the Wizard Wars in the Mica Land. But who slew the demon of Dwarn'ir?"

"Priot," the torchbearer said disinterestedly.

"Of course," said the swordsman. "I have it straight now. It was Priot at Dwarn'ir, Megis at Fruhs, Horin at Ogleefra, Hirag in the Mica Land. These are things we are all familiar with."

"Excuse me," I said.

The swordsman glanced down. "What is it?"

"Your foot is on my chest."

"I know," he said.

"I've been listening to you." My attitude was pious and unruffled. "You have a fine memory."

He grinned. "I seldom forget anything I hear."

"This is the prime quality of a scholar."

"I prefer fighting." He swung his sword in the torchlight, but I could see that he was flattered.

"The star you witnessed earlier was an omen," I said. "Do you seek to endeavor, to gain an end, to profit in your travels?"

"Who does not?" asked the torchbearer.

The swordsman said, "We drive our clarows to the market-place of Klask'an to sell."

"Success will greet you there," I said confidently.

"Tell us more," said the torchbearer with just the barest trace of cynicism in his voice.

I pressed on regardless. "Greater rewards than you expect await you, and your dealings will be with men of honor."

"You are certain of this?" said the swordsman.

"As certain as I am that I am mortal."

He hesitated, then smiled. "I believe you." He took his foot off my chest. "You are no demon."

"Bless you," I said with genuine fervor.

"He is no demon," the swordsman said loudly for the benefit of those in the last row. "He is but a mortal."

A figure pushed his way through the crowd, and came and stood over me. I stared up at him. He had the authoritative bearing of someone important.

"This may be a mortal and not a demon," he said. "But what sort of a mortal is he?"

"A simple kirlu," I said, "and nothing more."

"And riding a thoroughbred clarow," he said. "How did you come by such an excellent animal?"

"My family gave it to me when I entered Ytrifg's service," I said. "It was a going away present."

"Going away from where?"

"Klask'an."

"And now you are going back?"

"I have fasted and I have grown lean," I said. "Ytrifg came to me in a vision and bid me return. I am hungry and tired. I wish to eat and sleep. That is all."

"Are you aware of the fact that there are bandits in this desert as well as demons?"

"Yes."

"They attacked us once already tonight," he said. "And though we beat them off, they could still be near. Might they have sent a spy to us to determine our weaknesses?"

"I am not a bandit spy," I said.

"Can I be sure of that?"

He looked at me thoughtfully, and my death was on his face. That face scared me more than the blade at my throat did. Furthermore I was just about disgusted with lying on the ground and answering dumb accusations. But I had no choice, here in the midst of it. So I summoned up all my various hidden reserves of courage and patience and piety and so forth.

"I am not a demon," I said reasonably. "I am not a bandit spy. I am a kirlu. My life is my work, and my work is prayer. Ytrifg be praised."

"That may be true," he said. "All that you say may be true. But then again it may not be."

"I believe what he says," the swordsman said staunchly.

The authoritative one pursed his lips. "Then bind him, and

feed him, and watch him. We should see soon enough who he is."

The blade moved away from my throat, and the swordsman gestured for me to stand. When I was standing, he drove his sword into the sand, and held out his hands to me. I laid both my hands across his, and we gripped each other's wrists.

"My name is Protew," he said. "Yours is—?"

"Gnarla," I smiled at his fine memory.

"I recall it now." He indicated the authoritative one. "This is Weffsil, our leader."

"Eat and sleep," Weffsil said to me. "Tomorrow we go to Klask'an. You may ride there with us if you like."

"A privilege," I said.

"If you last out the night," he added.

Protew clapped my shoulder. "I'll give you something to unwrinkle your belly. Then you can tell me of your wanderings, and I can tell you of mine."

"You're on sentry duty," Weffsil reminded him.

Protew made an explosive noise and turned to me. "We can talk tomorrow, on the way to the city."

"Tomorrow," I said.

He clapped my shoulder again and strode away. A moment later he was back at his post on the shelf of rock. Weffsil conferred with the torchbearer, then brought him over to me.

"Soraft will see to your needs," he said, and went off.

"Food first, I suppose," Soraft said.

I nodded. "Please."

"How long did you fast for?"

"Many days," I said.

"Why?"

"It improves the quality of my visions."

"Have you ever tried wine?" he said.

"Once or twice."

"How were the visions then?"

"Unclear," I said.

His eyes glinted in the torchlight. "You're really very cleaver for a kirlu."

"Am I?"

"Aren't you?"

"I wouldn't know," I said.

"Most of the kirlus I've met were dull, with far more holiness than sense or wit, and you seem to have both."

I glanced around to change the subject. "What happened to my clarow?" Pacesetter was nowhere to be seen.

"He's being cared for." Someone came up and gave Soraft a length of rope and went away. "I have to tie you up now."

"Hand and foot?" I said.

"Just hand." He passed me his torch to hold, tied my hands in front of me, then took the torch back. "Too tight?"

I tested the ropes. "They're fine."

"Come along and we'll feed you."

"I appreciate it," I said.

He led me to a place next to the fire. A woman was squatting by the flames, roasting a chunk of meat on a stick. The juices from the meat hissed and sizzled as they drooled and fell into the fire. The odor of the meat was overpoweringly savory.

"For you," Soraft said.

"Smells delicious." I could hardly wait.

"Hey Meas," Peter's voice came in my head. *"You there?"*

"I'm here," I said.

Soraft looked at me. "What's that?"

"Praying thanks in my prayer language." I'd spoken to Peter in Basic, which the drover didn't understand.

"I'll leave you to it." Soraft went and dropped his torch in the fire and stood back watching me.

"He thinks you're really very clever."

I sat down tailor fashion on the ground. "For a kirlu."

"Probably a veiled insult."

"More likely a veiled innuendo."

"Meas the demon spy."

"So you heard all that."

"Every word." Peter had also taken a hypnocourse in Jsimaj's cultures et cetera. *"You're in with them now."*

"I hope so."

"They're buying you dinner."

"It's the least they can do after that inquisition."

"*Sure it is.*"

"I'd do the same for them."

"*Of course you would.*"

The woman by the fire came over and gave me the stick with the meat still impaled and dripping with succulence. Soraft returned and sat down tailor fashion beside me.

"Call again later," I said to the distant orbiting spaceship. "It's suppertime."

"*Enjoy.*" I could hear his transmitter click off.

I tore loose a piece of meat with my teeth, having just a little trouble with my false upper plate, which was kept in place only by suction. The meat was hot and rare. I couldn't remember when I'd last had anything that tasted quite so good.

Ghostly figures moved around the campfire, jittery shapes that murmured indistinctly. Music of a sort drifted by from a harsh atonal instrument that sounded something like a chanter. The melody, if there was one, escaped me.

I glanced over at my guard. In the firelight, his face was black. It had some humor, some strength, some curiosity. His cheekbones were high, his brow was heavy, his eyes set deep. He caught me staring at him and turned his head.

"I don't believe in demons," he said.

"Why not?"

"Because I've never seen one."

I took another bite of the meat. "Humph."

"Neither do I believe in gods." He apparently wanted us to have a theological debate.

"Believe what you will," I said, "and I'll do the same."

"The other kirlus I've met have tried to convert me."

"I'd rather eat."

"Your lord is who?" he said.

I had to gulp down my food in order to reply to him. "Ytrifg The Inscrutable."

"What does he demand of you?"

"Nothing," I said.

"Then what does he do himself?"

"We never discussed it."

"But he appeared to you recently in a vision," Soraft said. "He must have had something to discuss with you."

"He berated me for fasting so much, and suggested that I should go home and have fun."

"A nice lord."

I took another bite of the meat. "He suits me."

"Klask'an is your home?"

"Ummm." I was chewing. "Humm."

"How have things been there?"

"Ah er ah." The meat was spicy and a bit stringy, and I was making a complete slob of myself over it.

"Has the city grown strange lately?"

I pricked up my ears, and swallowed the meat. "Strange?"

"Like strange occurrences," he said.

"Occurrences?"

"Perhaps you left for the desert before they began."

"It's hard to be sure," I said. "Which strange occurrences?"

"The way I heard it—"

A drover ran up, waving a sword, gasping for breath, and halted in front of us. "The bandits are back."

"Plague on them." Soraft shot me a look.

"They're still trying to make off with a part of the herd," the drover panted. "We're holding them, but they're persistent."

Soraft stood up abruptly and drew his sword, then took my arm and forced me to stand up too. "Let's go and see."

"My meal," I said.

"It can wait."

I resisted him. "I'm a holy man, not a fighter."

"You can pray for our victory," he said.

Soraft followed the drover, into the moonlit darkness, dragging me right along with them.

We came out of the cliffrock box and into a full blast of wind. My next bite of meat was mainly sand. I spat it out. The meat on the stick was ruined. I threw it away in disgust. Grains of sand remained between my teeth, grinding them down and coating my tongue. My bells jingle jingled. We quickly lost sight of the drover up ahead of us.

There were hundreds of multipedes milling around nearby in the moonlight. They howled and wailed and stank beyond belief. We walked along the angled side of the mountain. The wind blew straight at us like a needle spray. I held my cowl shut over my nose. Soraft hung on to me tightly so we wouldn't get separated, and spoke above the noise of the animals and wind.

"They picked a fine time to raid," he said.

"Perfect." I spat out more sand.

"Hurry up."

"Take it easy." I pointed at a vague shape darting in and out among the multipedes. "Who's that?"

"One of ours."

"You can tell?"

"One of theirs would fear the clarows' claws," he said. "I liked the way you won over Protew earlier this evening."

"Did you?"

A multipede stepped too close. I jumped out of its way. Soraft jerked at my arm and my body half turned towards the mountainside. My cowl fell back. I averted my face from the wind and saw the attacker. Without hesitation I kicked Soraft's legs out from under him. He went down and the attacker sailed over him and past me with a curse. I got set.

The attacker rolled and started to rise. I pinned his sword hand to the ground with my sandaled foot. Then he started to do something with his other hand. I didn't feel like arguing with him about it. So I stomped on his throat hard with my other foot, and he expired with a couple of limp gurgles. Soraft stood up and stared down at the corpse, which was already partially buried in the sand.

"A bandit," he said.

"That's good.

"You disposed of him neatly."

"I always try to be neat," I said.

"But you denied that you were a fighter."

My stomach felt queasy. "This was a special case."

"I owe you my life."

"Forget it," I said.

I stooped over and peeled the bandit's fingers away from his sword. He was the first man I'd ever killed, and his toga had gotten rucked up around his waist. I pulled it decently down. His sword was weighty, and the hilt was thick, covered with multipede hide. I gave it to Soraft. The rope I was tied with made hefting it difficult.

"I guess you're not a bandit spy," Soraft said.

"Guess not."

He looked almost ashamed. "You can go back to camp and finish eating if you like."

"My appetite is gone."

"A pity."

"And I don't think I could find my way back in this wind," I said. "I haven't any sense of direction at all. Maybe I'd better stay with you, since you seem to know where you're going."

"Hold out your hands," he said.

I held them out. Soraft used the bandit's sword to cut the rope that bound me. I massaged my wrists. They weren't too bad. He'd been gentle when he'd tied me, though not the least bit careless. I glanced at him. His eyes met mine with a kind of skeptical candor. Then he gave me back the sword.

"For what?" I said.

"Just to carry."

"Oh."

"I have one of my own here," he said. "I can't manage the both of them comfortably."

The sword was an old one, deeply scarred by marks of combat. "All right."

"Just to carry."

"Sure," I said.

"Listen."

I listened. "A scream."

"And another," he said.

There came the ringing of steel against steel. We went forward again, towards the battle, into wind and sand. Once I tripped on an outjutting rock, but recovered before I fell. Then I stumbled into Soraft, who leaped aside with an oath.

"It's you," he said.

"Sorry."

"Bandits like to ambush people."

"I know," I said.

We went forward again, across a mad landscape, overly filled with multipedes, tinkling bells, shouts, clashes, and endless gritty sand. All of it came to us on a hot malignant wind, under a moon that froze the heated surfaces below to burning ice.

The herd was getting very skittish now. They were making more noise, another example of feedback. The nervousness of one animal was communicated to those nearest it. Their nervousness reinforced that of the others around them. This in turn recommunicated itself to the original beast with predictable results.

Shortly the leaders of the herd would bolt, and the rest would follow as a matter of course. It would make for a dandy stampede. I could picture the way it would happen, and wanted to be elsewhere when it did, particularly not in front of them.

Those hundreds of thundering terrorstruck armored tanks, with the vicious claws designed for rooting out food in the hostile desert, would simply annihilate anything that blocked the path of their escape route. The thought of it made me cringe.

"What's up down there?" Peter's voice was louder than the activity around me, and somehow much more real and immediate.

"Party time," I said softly.

"Is everyone having a ball?"

"You remember when we wondered whether it was drovers or bandits I had to contend with?"

"Yeah."

"It's both."

"So I've been noticing."

"You can't see us, can you, from way up there?"

"No but I sure as hell can hear you."

"Wait a minute."

A multipede had pinned me against the mountain. I hollered at him. He yowled at me. Soraft was nowhere to be seen. Then the multipede gave a bit. I climbed on his back, my robes a nuisance, and perched precariously. The mountain was to one side of me, a churning sea of multipedes to the other. I was trapped.

"*Meas?*"

"Later," I said.

"*Are you in trouble?*"

"Shush."

"*Is it—*"

"Don't distract me."

Without Soraft I was friendless. Most of the drovers probably still thought that I was a bandit spy. The bandits would probably think that I was a drover. A space appeared between the multipedes. I threw myself off the one I was on and into the opening.

Some desperate fancy footwork got me safely back to the side of the mountain. I drew in a breath and tried to blink the sand out of my eyes. The animal noise was deafening. But not quite deafening enough to drown out Peter's insistent voice.

"*I want to know what's happening.*"

"Later."

"*Are you okay?*"

"I'm okay," I said. "Oh Jesus."

A man stepped out from a patch of mountain shadow. His sword arm was raised. I tensed to strike and defend, my captured weapon heavy in my hand. He moved closer. I moved away, still blinking. And my vision cleared briefly. I saw who it was.

"Gnarla," he said.

My relief was profound. "Soraft."

"I was afraid I'd lost you."

"You almost did."

"The bandits have vanished again," he said. "But now we have an even worse problem."

"The herd." It was obvious since we were shouting above the wild commotion the animals were making. "They want to stampede."

He nodded. "The excitement has them stirred."

"That's bad."

"Very bad," he said. "Many of them would die in a stampede. The loss in revenue would be a disaster for my people. We can't drive dead clarows to market."

"And so?"

"To calm the herd we have to calm their guides."

I glanced around. "Where are these guides located?"

"At the front," he said. "Where else?"

"But what if they won't calm down?"

He made a gesture. "They run."

"Right over anyone who's in their way."

"It's a definite risk." He stared at me intently. "Will you help us calm them?"

"No," said my mind.

"Yes," said my tongue.

Soraft smiled. "I knew you would."

The terrain was a nightmare of sand and wind and anguished multipedes. Somehow we made it to the front. A squad of the drovers had assembled there, and were doing their best to calm the animals. It seemed to be working fairly well. At least the noise level had dropped some, or maybe I was just getting used to it.

Soraft went up to the nearest multipede and threw his arms around him. The animal began to quiet at once. Show them you care. So I did the same thing, caressing the horny snout of a rambunctious beast, until he stopped rearing and shrieking. By then my ears were numb to it anyway.

As soon as that one was calmed, I went on to the next. I gave him love and affection. He responded by not clawing me to death. I went on to the next one, and slowly the situation improved. As time passed the number of drovers up front diminished. I started to remember how tired and hungry and rotten I felt, and I wanted Soraft to specify those strange occurrences in Klask'an that he'd mentioned to me back at the campfire.

I looked around for him. He was standing less than fifteen meters away, his arm in the mouth of a multipede, speaking into the animal's auditory area. I was about to go and take care of my business with him, when I heard a yell and turned to see what was the matter. And I saw that the sonovabitching bastard bandits were launching yet another fucking attack against us.

There were seven of them and five of us. The wind wasn't blowing as hard now, and it was easy to count by the moonglow. The bandits had waited their charge until the herd was quiet, presumably because they didn't want a stampede any more than we did. Night was their ally. A stampede would have lasted past the light of day.

One of the bandits came at me. He was shouting, swinging his blade from side to side, parallel to the ground. I flung my captured sword at him like a javelin. It went into his chest heart high. He kept on coming, he kept on shouting, he kept on swinging his blade, unwilling to admit he was dead.

I sidestepped him as he went by, and kicked him just below the ribcage, hurting my toes in the process. He fell on his belly in the sand. Limping but still game, I went over to him, and rolled him on his back. He was done. I pulled my sword from his chest, wiped it on his toga, and surveyed the battlefield.

Two of our men were down, and two of the bandits, including mine. All the dead were a mess. With these double edged swords, you weren't equipped for subtleties. Mostly it was hack and chop and slice and slash. The method was sloppy, but it was also effective.

Another of our men was being worried by three of the bandits at once. He was doing pretty well though, because his assailants were just banging around, getting in each other's way. He was holding them off quite nicely.

Soraft was fighting with two more of them. As I watched, one of the bandits bought it, his skull cleft nearly in half. The other one danced back to reassess the situation. I went over and sort of cut the man down from behind. Soraft grinned at me and nodded, then pointed to the remainder of the battle.

It turned out I recognized the drover with the three assailants. He was Protew, my friend, the sentry. The three couldn't get anywhere near him. He was flexing his muscles, weaving a complex and murderous pattern in the air with his blade, and roaring with laughter. The bandits had to move fast to avoid him.

Soraft and I jumped into the fray. The three tried to regroup to meet us, but it was too late for that. Protew drove his sword to the hilt into one, and the bandit gave up the ghost with a groan. Soraft took a long leap forward, swung his sword over his head like an axe, and lost a hand to the bandit on his left.

The bandit collapsed as my own sword went in one side of him and out the other. Soraft was finished with the fight. He just stared at the stump of his wrist, fountaining blood as the arteries pumped it out, squirt squirt squirt squirt squirt. And then his eyes became sightless and he toppled over.

I knelt quickly at his side and tore my holy cord from around my waist. Using my sword to tighten it, I made a jingling tourniquet for the wound. Meanwhile Protew dispatched the final bandit alone with no trouble. The bandit never felt a thing. Protew simply knocked his sword aside and decapitated him.

I checked for a pulse in Soraft's right wrist. It was thin and ragged. He was in a state of shock. I checked his left wrist. The amputation had been reasonably neat, and he'd been lucky in the way he'd fallen. A minimum of sand had gotten into the raw open stump. I lifted up his head and put it in my lap.

"How is he?" Protew asked me.

"Hurt," I said.

"Will he live?"

"He might."

The drover who'd brought us the news of the attack back at the campfire hove into view. "It's over?"

"Vwen and Orin were killed," Protew said. "But we got the bandits. Tell Weffsil the kirlu fought with us."

"I will," the drover said. "I would have been here myself, but I thought they'd given up for the night."

Protew clapped his shoulder. "They've given up now."

"I can see that." The ground was strewn with bodies and parts of bodies. "How many were there?"

"Nine or ten," Protew said. "Maybe more."

"There were seven," I said.

Protew shrugged. "I was close."

"We can bury ours," the drover said. "The herd can take care of theirs tomorrow when we leave."

"Trampling's the best they should get." Protew began to walk in a circle and peer at the ground.

"Is Soraft hurt badly?" the drover asked me.

"He lost one hand in the fight." I indicated the stump and my makeshift tourniquet. "He needs some bandages."

"I'll go and get them," the drover said.

"Wait a minute before you go." Protew stooped to pick up something small and black. "Take this with you and burn it."

The drover squinted. "What is it?"

"Soraft's hand," Protew said.

"Are you certain it's his?" the drover asked.

Protew gave it to him. "I'm certain."

"So am I," I said.

Protew nodded. "Be sure and burn it."

"I will," said the drover.

"And don't forget the bandages," I said.

"I won't." The drover went off again.

Protew squatted beside me. "You use a sword well."

"Not as well as you."

"I practice a lot." He chuckled. "A kirlu with a sword."

"It isn't mine," I said. "And I hate it."

"You'd rather pray?"

"Much."

"I'd rather brawl," he said, "or make love."

My eyes were tired and sandy, and I felt like a cancelled stamp. "I don't hate making love."

"Then there's hope for you."

"I'm glad," I said.

A couple of drovers came and loaded Soraft onto a litter. Protew made sure that the tourniquet was kept tight. The second moon had appeared, and my mind began to drift with it. The first moon swam across my vision. I closed my eyes for just a moment, to rest them and blink away the sand. And the darkness rushed in on me all of a sudden, and everything up and dissolved while I wasn't looking.

Someone was moaning and someone was shaking me awake. I came up disoriented to a blare of heat and a glare of bright sunshine. I opened my eyes by degrees, letting the light fill them gradually. I saw a mass of mountain, black and brown and gray, and a stretch of intense yellow sand. The moans continued, moans of pain.

I turned and saw that it was Protew shaking me. Beyond him was a forest of clawfooted legs attached to a placid wall of pale green multipedes. There were piles and piles of dung, and tiny creatures were playing in the piles. I glanced upward, away from the stink. Carrion birds with crimson feathers were soaring around in a sky of bottomless blue.

I was sopping wet. The sand was everywhere, crawling up my thighs while the sweat dripped down them, crusted on my lips, clinging to my hair, embedded in my pores. I felt like a year of hard living and no respite. The moans went on. I licked my lips with an arid tongue, and that was a waste of my time.

"Are you thirsty?" Protew asked me.

"Unnhhnnhh."

He passed me a bulging water bag. "Drink this."

"Ahhhhhhh." I started to chugalug it. "Urrgh blouff oomphh." I slowed myself down. "Ahhhhhhh."

"Gnarla?" Protew said.

"Ummmm."

"Soraft is dying."

I corked the water bag. "Where is he?"

"Ccme on," Protew said.

He took the bag back, bent down and assisted me, tinkling softly, to my feet. Someone had been nice enough to bring back my bells. That was good. I'd have been noplace without them. Protew supported me with an arm like a block of wedgeroot. That was good too. I could hardly have stood on my own. The walk was a short one, but it exhausted me.

Soraft lay on the ground, thrashing about in pain, and moaning. He was unconscious. His stump was bound with a strip of cloth. He hammered the sand with it. I knelt down next to him and gripped his arms, trying to keep him from hurting himself any further. He arched his spine convulsively and twisted away from me.

"I can't hold him," I told Protew. "You'd better do it."

"All right."

"Let me have that water bag."

"Here," he said.

He passed me the bag again, then pinned Soraft to the ground. There were other strips of cloth lying about. I picked one up, shook the sand off it, and dampened it from the bag. Soraft's head was whipping back and forth. He kept moaning. I scrubbed at his face with the cloth, but that was useless to him. What he probably needed most that I could give him just then was a drink.

"Hold him steady," I said.

Protew grunted. "I'm doing my best."

"His head."

"Watch out." Protew straddled Soraft and held him that way while he took his ears. "I've got him."

"Hang on," I said. "But gently."

I poured a few drops of water between Soraft's open jaws. It bubbled out again. I poured some more. His throat worked as he swallowed it. I poured some more. About half was staying down, a pretty fair average. I felt his forehead. He was very hot. I couldn't be positive how much was fever and how much was caused by the broiling sun. Enough was fever, I thought, to concern me.

"We'll be moving out soon," Protew said.

"When?"

"As soon as camp is broken up."

"In an hour?" I said.

"A lot less."

I thought of another concern. "Did anyone—" there wasn't a word for cauterize in their vocabulary, and that was the answer to my question in itself "—put fire to this wound?"

"Fire?" Protew looked puzzled. "Why?"

So that gangrene, which was almost certain to prove fatal here, wouldn't set in. "Just asking."

"Is it something that should be done?"

"Too late," I said. "Forget it."

He frowned. "Isn't there anything we can do?"

"I wish there was."

"We have to do something," he said.

"Like what?"

He clenched his fists. "I don't know."

"Neither do I," I said.

We stared bleakly at each other. Around us the camp was a bustle of activity. Women were bundling things up, and stowing them on the backs of multipedes. Men were preparing the herd for travel, giving the animals water and sage advice. Children were running off in all directions, and generally getting in everyone's way. A drover rode up on a multipede and pulled to a halt before us.

"Are you ready to go?" he asked Protew.

Protew turned to me. "Well?"

"Well," I said.

"We can't wait for you," said the drover.

I glanced down at Soraft. His moaning had stopped for the most part, and Protew's bulk kept him from thrashing much. But I didn't like the idea of him going on a journey. In his condition it could easily kill him. I had to get to Klask'an myself, but a day's delay might save Soraft's life. And one day more or less would be no big loss to me. I made a decision.

"Can you stay here with Soraft and me?" I asked Protew.

"How long?"

"A day maybe."

He clapped my shoulder. "Of course I can stay."

"Maybe more than a day."

"As long as necessary." He turned to the multipede rider. "Tell Weffsil I'm staying with Soraft and the kirlu."

The rider nodded, wheeled his multipede in a tight circle, and rode back the way he'd come. Watching a multipede wheel about is a genuine experience. All those legs going at once, and apparently in different directions. It's simply amazing.

I gave Soraft more water. He got it down and his eyes opened, worn copper discs in an amber solution. They went one way and then the other, as though he sought escape. Then they rolled back in his head and the lids drooped. His entire body went limp.

"Get off him," I said.

Protew clambered off. "Is he dead?"

I felt for a pulse, and it was there, still thin and ragged, but there. "No he's resting."

"That's good for him." Protew took the water bag. "I'd better go and refill this." '

"And get food," I said. "I'm starving."

He promised that he would and left. I wiped my face on the damp cloth, and tried to think of something to do about gangrene. But I couldn't think of anything I could do with what was available to me here. There was stuff I could have used aboard the ship, but the ship was too far out of reach for me to reach it.

"Meas?" Peter's voice inside my skull seemed to be responding to a telepathic cue.

"Present," I said.

"Can you talk to me now?"

I got myself into a prayerful attitude, and bent down over Soraft's body. "I can talk."

"So let me in on what's been happening?"

I let him in on it. "It's just one of those things," I finished up, meaning the delay.

"Your trouble is that you get involved."

"My trouble is that I am involved," I said. "But enough of that. Where are you?"

"Straight up about two kilometers. Top of the morning. How about a cup of coffee?"

I felt a twinge. "Hypnotherapy has me off coffee and cigarettes for the duration."

"Hypnotherapy gives you a strength you don't have. But I don't need that strength. I can indulge myself. In fact I'm sipping a strawberry malted right this minute. Ummmm mmmmmm."

"You're a sadist." I had a weakness for strawberry malteds and he knew it. "Pipe some music down to me."

"Anything in particular?"

"Use your own judgment."

"The classics?"

"Whatever you like, but not loud."

"Okay."

A moment later my brain was full of Beatle music, which was being rediscovered that year. *Picture yourself in a boat on a river.* I saw Protew speaking with Weffsil. Occasionally they gestured in my direction. *Plasticine porters with looking glass ties.* Protew and Weffsil concluded their conversation, and Protew returned to where I was sitting.

"Weffsil agrees that we should stay here with Soraft," Protew said. "Our mounts are going to be left behind for us. I'll be back soon with food and water."

"Great," I said.

The ground shuddered. *All the lonely people, where do they all come from.* The herd was moving out. Protew went and got the food and water, pinched and patted a few of the women farewell, smacked one of the kids in the ass, and then came back and sat down beside me. *All the lonely people, where do they all belong.*

"Listen to this," Protew began enthusiastically.

I made a stopping gesture. "Wait just a second. I have to finish my prayers." I bent over the food. "Peter."

The music faded down. "*Yeah?*"

"Could you put on some instrumentals?"

"*Why?*"

"Those lyrics are too damn distracting."

"*At your service.*"

A symphony that I didn't recognize came on. I ate my breakfast. Protew launched into an extremely improbable tale about one of his amorous exploits. It concerned twin sisters, their mother, a female neighbor, and a very perverted mongrel dog. When I finished eating I told him the one about the man with the giant corkscrew penis. And then he told another, and so did I, and the music went round and round, and thus the morning passed into oblivion.

Soraft's sleep became restless. I asked Protew to take a walk. He wouldn't have quite understood the real reason, so I told him that I had a ritual to enact that required solitude. Having been impressed by all my earlier prayers, he went away to a place out of sight around the cliffside.

When he was gone, I took out my teeth. I extracted a styrette of pain killer, and one of stimulant, and I injected Soraft with both. His breathing grew less harsh. I put my teeth back in. His injured arm went out to the sand and dug a furrow. Then his eyes fluttered open, squinting at the deadly sun.

"What's happened to me?" he rasped in a voice like gravel grinding against gravel.

"An accident," I said gently. "A mischance."

"The herd?"

"On its way to Klask'an." I smiled at him. "We'll be rejoining it shortly, when you're ready to travel."

"I'm ready now." He tried to sit up, his face contorting with the effort.

I pushed him back. "Easy there."

"The bandits," he said. "Did we get them?"

"We got them."

"My arm hurts and I feel—" He held up his arm, and his eyes went wild. "My hand. I can feel it, but it's not there. I make a fist, but—"

"You lost it to one of the bandits," I said. "In exchange he lost his life."

Soraft lay back again, his expression resigned. "So now I have only one hand. I am no longer complete."

I offered him the water bag. He drank from it greedily. I suggested food, but he refused. Then Pacesetter came over and nudged me with his snout. I offered him some water too. He guzzled it and snorted his appreciation, then went back by the other two animals, to help them graze among the spikey desert plants. I watched them for a while.

Their pale green hides were oddly aquatic in the heat shimmer. A haze was over everything. On the horizon the blue sky melted down to the desert, and the desert rose in waves of yellow to meet it. My pores were so open that it seemed as though I was melting too. I turned back to Soraft. He was staring at his stump, and probing it with his good left hand.

"You mentioned strange occurrences in the city," I said for the information, and to divert him from his wound.

"I've heard rumors," he said slowly, still probing.

"For example?"

"They say the Derone has troops in the streets and is recruiting an army."

I drummed my fingers against my leg to the beat of the music in my brain. "He had an army before."

"That's true," Soraft said. "But an army of peace for defense of the city. This is an army of conquest. They say the Derone plans to pay them in booty."

"Do they say why the change?"

Soraft nodded. "They say the Derone has new advisors, not from this part of the world."

"From where then?"

He glanced at me shrewdly. "Perhaps from the same place that you come from."

"*Gapjumpers advising the Derone,*" Peter said.

"Sounds like it," I agreed in Basic.

"*Our presence here becomes all nice and legal.*"

"Which represents an advance of sorts." To Soraft I said, "A charm to keep the poisonous spirits in your body at bay."

"Thank you." His expression was thoughtful.

Peter giggled. "*Dirty old gapjumpers.*"

"We'll see," I said.

Gapjumpers are people who enter a primitive society and jump the technological gap, accelerating development faster than the host culture can tolerate. The culture breaks up under the strain, and the gapjumpers step in and take over. And Jsimaj had a large enough supply of radioactives to make it worth owning.

We now had a perfectly valid excuse for being here. The Great and General Council, of which CROWN was a member, was foursquare against the business of gapjumping. But we could claim we were here to save this planet, even if we had to take it into protective custody to do so. Deceit is the essence of deceit.

"I don't believe," Soraft said to me, "that you're either a demon or a bandit spy."

"I'm not."

"But I also don't believe that you're a kirlu."

"Does it matter?" I said.

He looked up at the crimson carrion birds that were soaring in the sky. "Does it?"

"No."

"All right," he said.

I sighed. "There's something I want to know. Did those rumors you heard include any sort of talk about unusual weapons for the new army?"

"Unusual in what way?"

"In the way of being better or more efficient?"

"Not that I can recall," he said.

"Oh well."

"*Hey Meas?*"

"Ummmm."

"*Find out whether—*"

"Hold it," I said.

"*I was—*"

"Shhhh."

Protew had just come running around a corner of the cliffside. "Riders approach us from the direction of the city."

"Who are they?" I asked.

"Bandits maybe," Protew said, "seeking revenge."

"*Problems problems problems.*"

"How many?" Soraft asked.

"I'm not exactly sure." Protew drew his blade. "They're raising a lot of dust."

"*There's over thirty.*"

I grimaced. "We can't hold them off."

"But we can make their vengeance costly," Protew said.

"*Or you could hide.*"

"Best idea of the day," I subvocalized.

"*Consider the source.*"

"That was the first time I ever subvocalized," I said astonishedly, doing it again. "The only one that can hear me is you."

"*I'm thrilled beyond measure.*"

Soraft was feeling around with his good left hand. "Has anyone seen my sword?"

"Couldn't those riders be friendly?" I asked.

"*Hah.*"

"It's possible," Soraft said. "Where's my sword?"

"You just try to relax," I told him. "In our situation, we ought to negotiate, not start trouble."

Protew grinned and swung his blade in a sunlit silver arc. "I negotiate with this."

"With what?"

"A cutting edge," I subvocalized.

"That's what I thought."

"Damn it to hell," I said. "Nobody but you can hear me, but everybody can see me. My lips are still moving."

"Nail them shut."

"A sword," Soraft said. "Any sword."

I gave him the one I'd captured last night. He used it as a crutch to get himself to his feet. I had to take his arm to keep him from falling over. Protew swung his own blade repeatedly, like the scythe of a gay grim reaper. My bells jingled softly as Soraft leaned against me. Let the bastards come at us, we were ready for them. Peter put on another symphony. Now he was playing Saint-Saéns' *Danse Macabre*. I hummed along, slightly off key. But at least I didn't move my lips while I was doing it.

Protew died with a crossbow quarrel in his heart. His blade went point down, stuck in the sand, and Protew collapsed beside it, just like that. The men on the multipedes rode up near the corpse and reined in. Soraft and I were standing further back. The riders stared at us malevolently, but made no attempts to strike at us.

"Drop your sword," I said quietly.

Soraft dropped it. "You were talking about unusual weapons. What kind of arrow is that?" He pointed at the quarrel.

"A special sort of arrow," I said. "Do you know who these people are?"

"The Derone's soldiers, looking for blood."

"They found it."

"Surrender," called a soldier in the lead.

"We mean you no harm." I indicated Soraft. "This man is badly wounded. I'm but a peace loving kirlu."

"I want to sit down," Soraft said. "My legs are weak."

"So are mine," I said.

He sat down again. I squeezed his arm and took the ten or fifteen steps to where the corpse lay. Routinely I knelt and checked for a pulse. It was useless. The wide open eyes told the story, the filmed zero eyes that saw nothing. I pulled the quarrel from his chest and threw it away. There was something harsh and bitter in my throat, something scared and angry that I couldn't quite swallow. All the soldiers remained on their multipedes in tableaux.

"*What happened?*" Peter's voice was insistent.

"Protew is dead." The words were an effort. "They fucking killed him with a crossbow bolt."

"*Gapjumping technology.*"

I closed Protew's eyes, an eerie tactile sensation. "He never had a chance."

"*Are they going to kill you next?*"

"Shhhh."

The soldier who'd called to us to surrender had dismounted from his multipede. The troops waited silently behind him with their crossbows aimed at me. He paced out the distance between us in a military manner, as though he was marching on parade. He had a plume of red in his helmet that none of the others had. His face was stern, the face of a career officer, very cold and remote. He was clean shaven, of medium build. I could have broken his neck in a sixth of a second. When he reached me he stopped, and we both stared down at the corpse.

"He was threatening us," the officer said finally.

"Sure he was," I said. "There's no telling how much damage he might have done to you and your men with his blade from way over here. Do you mind if I bury him?"

The officer stiffened. "We can do that."

"You're far too kind."

He made a sharp motion. A pair of soldiers detached themselves from the group study and joined us. The officer ordered them to dig a hole and dig it deep, so that no desert creatures would uncover the corpse and defile it. They began to hollow out the sand with their swords. The officer gave me a small formal nod.

"You have the most profuse apologies of the Derone for this unfortunate incident," he said.

"Make your apologies to him," I waved at the corpse. "No doubt he will find them a solace."

The officer's face was expressionless. "I am Captain Gangot. We are here to investigate an abnormality."

"*I bet it's the ship.*"

"Ummmm," I said.

Gangot was saying, "Last night a star was seen to have fallen in the desert."

"*I win the bet.*"

"According to witnesses," Gangot continued, "the star returned to the sky at once. Did you observe this?"

"*You should have parachuted in or something.*"

"I observed it," I said. "But I assumed that it was merely an omen from my lord deity."

"Which deity?"

"Ytrifg The Inscrutable."

"The god with no features," Gangot said. "Has he communicated with you in this way before?"

I shook my head. "Generally he comes in dreams."

"Do you think you could guide us to the spot where the star fell?" Gangot asked.

"I don't know," I said.

"*You could guide them away from the spot.*"

"The Derone would be grateful for such a service," Gangot said. "You would be well rewarded for it."

"*Sold.*"

I gestured towards Soraft, who was watching us keenly. "That man is wounded, and shouldn't be left alone."

"These two can stay back to take care of him." Gangot meant the gravedigging detail. "What is his wound?"

"He lost a hand fighting bandits last night," I said. "He's a drover. The bandits came to steal from his herd, which is on its way to the city. The bandits are food for the desert now."

"They deserve no better," Gangot said. "Will you show us to the spot where the star fell?"

"*Show them, show them.*"

"I'll try," I said.

Gangot gave me another small formal nod. "We can provide you with a clarow to ride."

"I have one."

"Then let us leave immediately," he said.

"May I speak with the drover first?"

"Of course." Gangot went to confer with the burial squad. Walking back to Soraft I said, "Peter."

"*He isn't here.*"

"Get him."

"*Oh Peter.*" A pause. "*He's coming.*" A pause. "*Hello.*"

"I'd like you to do me a favor."

"*Name it.*"

"I'm serious about this."

"*Go ahead.*"

"I want you to stop all your talking to me when I'm talking to somebody, because it derails my train of thought and increases the danger I'm in."

"*Yeah.*" His tone was surly. "*Okay.*"

"I haven't any cutout switch for my end of the radio, and when I hear you I can't hear anything else."

"*I said okay.*"

"Okay."

Soraft greeted me. "Have we been taken prisoner?"

"I guess you could say that." I squatted beside him. "I have to go off with them for a while."

"To where?"

"They insist that I show them the spot where the star fell last night." I pointed to the three by the hole. "The two digging will stay with you until I get back. The one with the plume is Captain Gangot. He apologised for Protew getting killed."

"Did you accept the apology?"

"It wasn't my place to accept it."

"Those cursed soldiers," Soraft said.

"Don't give them any trouble."

He lifted his stump. "Not likely."

"We'll be pushing on to the city as soon as my little side trip is over with."

"Good."

Gangot had mounted his multipede. "Time to go, kirlu."

"I'm off." I started to rise.

Soraft touched my arm. "I've been noticing the devices on the backs of their clarows. Have you ever seen anything like them before?"

"No," I said.

But I had seen such things before. They were saddles with stirrups for the feet. And wars had been won because one side had saddles and stirrups to give them more stability on their steeds, and to allow them to ride faster and longer and harder and further. This was still more evidence of gapjumper technology. The improvements they made didn't have to be large, just large enough to accomplish their end. Superior weapons, superior transport, that was enough. The world could be theirs for the taking.

"You can't trust them," Soraft told me with a glance towards the mounted troop of soldiers.

"I won't," I said.

"They need you." His eyes were closing. "But they're treacherous." He was nearly asleep. "They have no mercy."

"I've seen that."

"Be careful."

"I will," I said. "I promise."

"Whoever you are." His head lolled. "Whoev—" His voice trailed away to a mumble.

"Kirlu," Gangot called. "It's time."

I got up, collected Pacesetter, and climbed aboard.

Captain Gangot moved along fast with his saddled men, and I kept up as best I could on my blanket. Dust from their multipedes choked me. I turned my face away from it. The sky was blind and empty, except for the deadly sun. Heat still shimmered on the horizon, and rose in waves from the molten sand. The sweat poured out of me. I felt like I was encased in a portable sauna. But Peter had put on a lilting harpsichord suite by Bach, and the music was very persuasive, made my physical situation seem vaguely unreal.

I could hardly remember having ever been cool. This heat was my heritage and my destiny, and endless vastness was my only home. The desert ahead and behind was laid out in a sequence of neat striations, as though someone had just passed through it with a rake a thousand kilometers wide. We were cutting a ragged diagonal path across these wind runes, and the almost occult precision of it all added strength to my feelings of unreality.

Pacesetter swayed

       swayed

swayed
    swayed
swayed.

I tried to think out my situation. Our man on Jsimaj, the missing Jules Atherton, was no longer the only factor. I still had to learn, if I could, what had happened to him. But I was fairly certain his fate was involved with the gapjumpers. Their presence here changed the entire attitude of my mission, though I wasn't yet sure how that change would ultimately affect me.

The bough of Pacesetter's back was lulling me, and without the Bach I would have dozed off. As it was, it was difficult to think. But one thing at least was clear. This development had compromised me. My disguise would fail to stand up under any kind of close scrutiny, because I couldn't give a satisfactory account of myself to anybody who really wanted one. Furthermore I'd been discovered at the scene, and the bad guys were going to ask me questions. They would be questions that I had no way of answering.

"Peter," I said. "You there?"

"I'm here." His tone was still surly. *"What's up?"*

I went through my chain of reasoning for him. "And I have to make a decision about what to do."

"So make it."

"Any suggestions?"

"Not me."

"None at all?"

"You're where the action is, and you have to solve your problems yourself. I've only been getting bits and pieces up here. My side of the picture is dim."

I considered for a moment. "You know that campsite where I spent the night?"

"Uh huh."

"And you know Soraft, the drover I met there?"

"Mmmmmm."

"I want you to pick him up," I said. "He'll probably die without some decent medical attention, which the shipsurgeon can provide for him."

"I can't let the natives see me. It's against the treaty rules, and my regulations forbid it."

"The hell with the goddam rules."

"This is my ship." Peter's voice had an edge. *"I'm not going to break regulations to save your friend from death. A lot of people may die before this is over with, and you might just as well resign yourself to the idea."*

"Pretty heartless, aren't you, up in your spaceship, removed from the blood?" My voice was edgy too, and I took a deep breath.

"If that's what you—"

"Listen to me," I said more evenly. "We're getting noplace. Let's begin again with a basic fact. The finger of suspicion has to be pointed away from me. Do you agree with that so far?"

"Yeah." His tone was grudging. *"So far."*

"All right." I coughed from the dust of the thirty multipedes I was following and went on. "There's two soldiers standing watch over Soraft. You land, kill them both, pick him up, take off. Who will everybody assume is the CROWN agent?"

"Who?"

"Soraft of course."

"But will everybody really assume that?"

"Maybe they won't," I said. "But it makes sense."

"Assuming that everybody assumes he's the CROWN agent, why will they assume that I picked him up?"

"Because of his wound."

There was a pause. *"This smacks of improvisation."*

"It is."

"You're inciting me to break the rules."

"That's life."

Peter sighed like a minor monsoon in my skull. *"Okay, Meas, I'm sold. It makes sense, it could work."*

"And you'll do it?"

"I'll do it."

"How soon can you get there?"

"I'm on my way."

His transmitter clicked off, and the music swelled. I caught up with the rearmost soldier, and told him to pass the word forward to Captain Gangot, that we were almost at the spot where I estimated the star had fallen. He tapped his multipede's auditory surface twice, and began to thread his way up the line. I pulled darling Pacesetter to a stop and waited, more glad for the chance to rest than I was about anything else.

Gangot made his way back to me. I told him I recognized the place we were at by the distinctive growth pattern of a group of cacti. They would have been a nearly perfect rhombus if connected like dots. Gangot motioned to his soldiers and ordered them to disperse and search the area. The men spread out.

"What are you looking for exactly?" I asked him.

"Heat signs, fused sand, burnt plants," he said. "Were you very close to the star when it fell?"

"I couldn't actually say for sure since I was prostrated in rapt adoration at the time."

Gangot gave me a narrow impatient stare. "Could you say which direction it came from?"

"Somewhere over there." I gestured at the mountains. "Not more than a short ride."

Gangot sent his men that way. I examined his saddle. It was a high boxlike affair with a sloped back and front that resembled a medieval jousting saddle. Suddenly a soldier cried out. Gangot and I turned towards him. He was turned towards the campsite we'd just left. The *Shoten Zenjin*, hull ablaze in the sunlight, jets aflare, retros athunder, was landing.

I threw myself off Pacesetter and buried my face in the sand, calling out the name of Ytrifg and beseeching his mercy. Most of the soldiers took their lead from me and commenced to behave in a similar fashion. Of course most of them were calling out the names of different gods than mine. But it's always nice to have a choice in these matters.

"Get up, you fools," Gangot shouted. "You stupid old women, you cowering clarows."

"Ytrifg Ytrifg Ytrifg," I prayed loudly. "Your power is great and I am but the humblest of your servants."

"Idiots," Gangot bellowed. "Imbeciles."

"Molofa," prayed a soldier.

"Ablegglego," prayed another.

"Ytrifg."

"Skalapant."

"Ytrifg."

"Ablegglego."

"Cospinase."

I felt a kick in my side. It was Gangot, quite furious. He snapped out an insult and moved on to his men, distributing blows and derogations with equal fervor. I continued to pray to Ytrifg, and I think I made a few converts. His name was invoked with an increasing frequency. Gangot returned to me. I knew this because I felt another kick. My face was back in the sand again.

"Be silent, kirlu, be silent," he said harshly. "What you see is but a natural thing."

I was obstinate. "Ytrifg Ytrifg Ytrifg. Allow me to comprehend your will and do your bidding."

"You make my men forget themselves," Gangot grated. "Be silent or I swear it will be your death."

That was enough for me. Remaining prostrate I shut off the flow, and after some effort Gangot managed to get his troops together. We mounted our multipedes, and started back to the campsite. I lagged behind as usual. We hadn't gone far when the *Shoten Zenjin* rose on her jets, and took once more to the bottomless sky. Presently I heard Peter's voice.

"Mission accomplished."

"Any trouble?"

"Nope."

"No hassle with the guards?"

"On the contrary. They were forthright and cooperative. At the sight of the ship, they fainted dead away."

"A commendable reaction."

"I liked it so much that I left them alive."

"Did you now?"

"Uh huh. I decided it was better than killing them. Let them report what they saw. It's to our advantage."

"In other words you couldn't bear to take their lives."

"Those are your words, not mine. I did what I felt was required of me under the circumstances."

"And the hell with the rules against them seeing you."

"Change the subject."

I grinned to myself. "Okay Peter my lad. I won't argue with you about it. How's Soraft doing?"

"Pretty well. He didn't seem too surprised when I told him I was acting on your behalf. There was one thing that did seem to bother him though."

"Which was?"

"My white skin. He wanted to know if it was some sort of fatal disease or something."

"I hope you told him the truth," I said with a mild trace of malice. "That there have been times, in the past, when white skins were fatal, for people with black skins."

"Meas." His tone was condescending. *"You mustn't be bitter. The past is past, over and done with, and nothing to do with you."*

"History is history."

"Bullshit is bullshit."

"A tautology's a tautology." I was feeling rather good. "You'd best keep careful track of your flank from now on. Doubtless the enemy has a ship too, and probably, or possibly, even several, and he, or they, might try to get at you with it, or them, as the case may be, so to speak, as it were."

"Repeat that slowly."

"What I mean is, watch your ass."

He laughed. *"Don't worry. I've been on security scan since we entered this system relativistically."*

"Just make sure you stay out of their way," I said. "I'm certain they'd take great pleasure in gunning down an unarmed ship."

"There's something else. You weren't told, I guess. It happens we're carrying ordnance up here."

I coughed from dust. "CROWN contact ships aren't supposed to fight. What price the rules, the mystic regulations?"

"What price indeed."

"Lightning will strike you."

"It'll strike us both."

"Whoosh."

"Zap."

A wind was rising again, this time fortuitous, blowing the sand, the troop dust, away from me. "Any other business?"

"Soraft wants to talk to you."

"Put him on."

"One moment." A pause. *"Go ahead."*

"Into this?" Soraft's voice was hesitant.

I could almost see Peter nodding. *"That's right."*

"Gnarla?"

"Yes Soraft I'm here," I said very gently. "Everything's going to be fine."

"I believe that. I must believe that. But also I must ask. Are you a demon?"

"Would it matter now if I were?"

"Please answer."

"No I am not a demon."

"I had to hear it once more. This child has done something to my arm where the hand was cut off. Now I feel weary, but the pain is gone. Will I see you soon?"

"I hope so."

"Will I see my people soon?"

"Not for a while," I said. "First there are things that have to be taken care of. Peter will explain our problem to you. He can also answer any further questions you may have."

"Unnhh."

"Soraft?"

"He's asleep," Peter said. *"I gave him a sedative along with the antibiotics. While he's resting I'll have to have the shipsurgeon shave off a little more of his arm and clean it up some. The whole thing is one big festering mass of pus. I can't imagine how it got so badly infected so fast."*

"The heat."

"I suppose."

"His piss poor diet."

"Yeah."

"Low resistance."

"Sure."

"Improper attention."

"Uh huh," Peter sighed.

"Well I have to go and square him away now. Keep in

touch. Is there any particular kind of music you'd like to hear?"

"Something lively," I said. "I have a long ride ahead of me, and I ought to stay awake for it."

"The Ecstasy Pipeline doing SHAWMUT BOULEVARD."

"That's a bit too lively."

"You've got it anyway."

His transmitter clicked off, and the music came on. It was like riding through a soundstorm, but after a couple of minutes I sort of got used to it. The desert contrived to reduce sensation to the bare essentials. Heat sand sway heat sky sway heat wind sway heat sun sway, with the music above and within it all and the distant tinkle of bells beyond. And at length I caught up with Gangot and his men at the campsite.

The two guards Gangot had left behind were in a state of gibbering panic. The officer was standing there trying to get a coherent story out of them and apparently failing dismally. The sand nearby was clearly scored by marks of the ship's landing, and all was in a fine feathered flurry of confusion. I dismounted from Pacesetter and knelt to the scorched ground. A good holy man should be prepared to pray at a moment's notice. Shortly Gangot came over and prodded me with his foot.

"Our search is ended," he said. "You'll be riding to the city with us as a special witness. Finish up your nonsense, and get ready to go."

I finished up and stood. "This has been a time of great wonders. How can you not believe?"

"By not believing." His gaze was directly upon me. "I'd like to know about that wounded man we left here."

"Know what?"

"Whatever you can tell." Gangot's face was intent.

I shrugged. "I never saw him before last night. I thought he was with the drovers. He was hurt. I was caring for him."

"Why?"

"Because he needed care."

Gangot's expression softened slightly. "Yes the sick, the weak, the defenseless, should be protected."

"An odd thing to hear from one who makes war."

"Some make war to have peace," he said. "Some have a different excuse. What about the man we killed?"

"What about him?"

"Who was he?"

"He also claimed to be a drover," I said. "I don't see the wounded man around here any more. Did he die?"

Gangot grunted. "Seemingly Ytrifg or one of those took him along to the sky. It must be marvelous to be on such friendly terms with the gods. Are you ready to leave?"

"I'm ready."

"Mount up," he said.

He turned on his heel and paced to his multipede, with his red plume waving in the breeze. I put my arm in Pacesetter's mouth for a brief exchange of love. Then I mounted up and tried to get comfortable, though the likelihood of that was very frail. While I was arranging myself, Gangot mounted his own multipede, and called to his men.

Two of them, not the same two who'd seen the ship land, rode over to me. They explained that their orders were to see that I didn't get lost. I thanked them for their concern. They took up positions on either side of me. We moved out again, across the desert, the wind runes, into the wind. I pulled my cowl shut and bore it stoically. A hundred or more years later we reached the city. It was really about fucking time.

Flashback I

The BETA building, Bureau of Extraterrestrial Administrations, on Earth, is huge and complex, a massive hexagonal
puzzlebox, standing some five hundred storeys high, and
covering more than ninety acres. It has nearly eight thousand
kilometers of corridor, and several million permanent em-
ployees. The structure encloses a gigantic park, with real
trees and flowers, picnic areas, fountains, memorial statuary,
playing fields, outdoor conference stations, and shaded walks
and bowers. Within the building itself, there are restaurants,
theatres, beauty parlors, gaming halls, shopping malls, ball-
rooms, classrooms, offices, labs, residential facilities, and
security guards. There are lots and lots of security guards.

One of these led me by a devious and confusing route to a
floor of the building so high that my ears popped long before
we actually got there. He deposited me in front of a door
with no lettering on it. The door slid back soundlessly. I
stepped through, not bothering to say see you later to my
escort, who remained outside. The office was small, done
completely in forest green, very restful to the eyes. Other
than a table, and the four men who were seated around it,
the room was empty.

Behind the table was a large picture window that took up

most of the wall. It showed a magnificent view of the
rechanneled Hudson River, and of the rocket pits beyond. As
I watched, a shuttle flared off from its webwork steel cradle,
and before it had been fully gulped down by the charcoal
gray sky, another had followed it, and another and another.
They swam in a steady endless stream. Out of sight from
where I stood, I knew that more rockets were landing and
unloading cargo, and then being returned to the takeoff area
on big electric carts. They were the vital links in the lifechain
of this depleted planet.

The four men stared at me.

I stared back at them.

We all stared at each other.

Then one of the men told me to sit. I was wondering
where my chair was, when it snuck up on me from the rear,
and tapped me on the insides of my knees. I sat, and the chair,
without so much as a by your leave, immediately clasped me
like a lover. I don't like such chairs. They're too goddam
pushy.

One of the men offered a cigar to me.

I refused.

All four of them lit cigars.

I lit a cigarette.

We would probably never be pals.

Behind them the distracting window polarized to forest
green. The lights in the room grew dimmer and more inti-
mate. Now we all sat for a while and smoked what we were
smoking and didn't look at each other. None of us said
anything. The smoke floated upward and disappeared into the
ventilation ducts.

I crossed my legs. There was a rustle of movement at the
table. Papers were being passed around. I crossed my legs the
other way. Somebody sighed. My cigarette burned to the end.
I put it out in the ashvac in the arm of my chair. The chair
shifted under me. I lit another cigarette.

One of the men began to speak, as though to himself. His
topic was entropy, the constant need for power. It may have
been that his topic was power, and entropy entered into it
only because it was there. He went on and on and on. His

best and final line was, freedon corrupts, and absolute freedom corrupts absolutely.

The other three men laughed at that.

I lit another cigarette.

My chair squirmed a bit.

The walls and ceiling in the room had been subtly chang-
ing color, taking on a deeper more serious hue to match the
tone of the speaker's voice. Now they were a dark and
somber olive green, the height of psychological manipulation.
I laughed at that. The four men leaned toward me and
glared, the cigars slanting out from between their fingers,
malign and absurdly phallic. The indirect lighting washed
away shadows. Their dull and unremarkable features were
blank and somehow remotely sinister. I think I was supposed
to be intimidated.

A second man began to speak. His topic was the ancient
Roman Empire, and how its very strength was its greatest
failing. It was so far flung that it couldn't reasonably govern
its provinces. So it let its provinces, in effect, govern themselves, and pay a tribute to Caesar, who tried to simplify
matters still further, by declaring that he was divine. I was
tremendously impressed by all this data.

A third man picked up the thread. He explained that, in
broad terms, CROWN, the Coalition of Registered Official
World Nations, had done the same thing as the ancient
Roman Empire. But CROWN had also tried to learn from
the past, and to apply its accumulated wisdom to the present.
CROWN did not pretend to be divine. And when CROWN
expanded territorially, this was done with the utmost deliber-
ation.

The first man waved his cigar at me.

I waved my cigarette at him.

My chair caressed my testicles.

The other men settled back.

The first man said that there was a planet, locally named
Jsimaj, that I'd likely never heard of. To CROWN it was just
a number in a star catalogue. That was today. Tomorrow, he
said, in the future, Jsimaj could become crucial, a pivotal
world, as a source of radioactives. He told me, without
mincing words, that Bloomer wouldn't last forever, not at

our present rate of energy consumption, nor would Byron, Hare Rama, Alexei, Cordella, or Dammitall. Entropy was catching at our coattails. Good old entropy. There were projections on just how long we could hold out against it, but the important thing was that we couldn't hold out indefinitely. That was definite.

The walls and ceiling shaded to emerald green.

It was time for the pitch.

I lit two more cigarettes simultaneously to prepare myself, and crossed and uncrossed and recrossed my legs six times.

My chair clutched me tighter.

The first man became totally earnest. He told me how important I could be in ensuring that nothing happened to Jsimaj that might compromise it in the future, the indefinite definite future when my own Coalition of Registered Official World Nations more than anyone else would have use for its resources. There were others less couth than CROWN, who might try to grab the place prematurely, plucking it from the vine before the true season of harvest. An agent of ours there had recently gone out of contact. This strongly indicated a dangerous enemy presence.

He explained to me the need for somebody new, somebody that no one recognized, a stranger to this type of operation. My special training in industrial espionage would fit me perfectly for the job. The fact that I'd been imprisoned once for illegal information retrieval wouldn't be held against me. He further pointed out the need for somebody with the right physical characteristics. I could easily pass for a native of Jsimaj and not be noticed. Then he offered me a million after taxes, a sum that I could get by on for the rest of my life. Finally he mentioned that a part of my sentence for illegal information retrieval still remained to be served. The mere mention of this was not in any way to be construed as a threat. But—

I accepted the job. My chair let me go. For some obscure reason, that made me feel rejected. It didn't matter though. The job didn't matter. Their blandishments here didn't matter. Nothing mattered much. I was numb inside. And they knew that. They knew that and they used their knowledge to twist me to their ends. It didn't matter though. I had to do something anyway. Brooding was senseless. Suicide was out of the question. I couldn't live with myself if I committed suicide. That much mattered. I was numb inside, but I wasn't dead. Mainly I had to have something to engage me from this moment to the next, something I could get lost in until my wheels and gears went back to turning from within again. This job would do as well as anything.

They gave me a temporary civil service rating and a contract, neither of which related to what I'd been hired for, but which the accounting department required as documentation.

They instructed me in armed and unarmed combat.

They indoctrinated me into some of the intricacies of political theory and interplanetary law.

They crammed me with an intensive hypnocourse in the languages, customs, history, and geography of the planet Jsimaj.

They replaced my teeth with new ones.

They taught me how to ride Earth's only multipede, one which had been brought in as a baby from Jsimaj years ago for study, then donated to a children's zoo, then requisitioned out of the cage to be mine all mine.

They used hypnotherapy to get rid of my craving for caffeine and nicotine, a treatment the therapist jokingly referred to as a form of abstract castration.

They pronounced me ready.

They assigned me a ship and a pilot.

And I left.

Part Two: The Message

We topped a dune, looked down, and there it was, the city. I'd come a long way, getting to this place, what with one thing and another. And now that I was here, more or less, I had to admit, it wasn't much. I stared at it while the score from *The Mikado* played through my brain.

Salt smells were blowing in from the ocean, along with the usual buckets of sand. The sun was still too hot. But somewhere along the way, I'd slid through exhaustion, and acquired the will to go on. Gangot's two soldiers were kind enough to remain on either side of me just to make sure.

Klask'an was made up entirely of squares. Some of them were higher than the others, but all were monotonous in their regularity of design. Standing there under the withering heat of the sun had driven all color from the city, if there had ever been any sort of color to it to begin with. Klask'an seemed like a toy construct, soap powder and chalk dust, transitory in its ultimate nature.

It made me think that men were born here, grew up and old, built things and tore things down, ate and slept, loved and killed their fellows, envolved their philosophies, followed their codes of conduct, laid their plans, lied and sought truth, struggled to survive, when in the end, in the end, when it

61

came to the end, the inevitable and unknowable end, the wind would blow, and the sand would cover everything for always.

The Lord High Executioner was singing that he had a little list. Well I had a little list too, and if my list got any worse, I'd just tumble off Pacesetter's back completely, and fall in a horribly crumpled heap at his feet, all twelve of them. I straightened up, took a deep breath, and willed my will to be willing. There was scenery here to be seen.

Contrasting with the lack of color presented by the city, were the trees and planted fields that surrounded it with green and brown. The bright slash of the River of Peace cut a swath through the volcanic ashpit, and the sparkling blue and white façade of the sea ran swift to the speechless horizon.

High buttresses had been erected where the land around Klask'an dipped into the sea. This was because of the planet's two moons, which at certain times created incredible swells of surf. It was the main reason why the city didn't extend all the way out onto the peninsula, but rather had turned itself back into the desert to spread. Most of the time a fair percentage of the peninsula was submerged, and water travel here tended to be limited, at least where the oceans were concerned.

Out in the fields men were at labor. They tilled the ground with tools that I couldn't identify at this distance. Other men stood over them. Multipedes were yoked together like oxen, pulling heavy equipment, ploughing the soil. Bright tendrils of water marked out irrigation ditches. To my left and ahead, where the mountains fell off in a series of jagged peaks, eventually becoming almost level on the desert floor, some sort of excavation work was in progress. The tunnel that brought the river through the mountain was only a short way from there. While I was taking all this in, Gangot rode up and halted beside me. I indicated the excavators.

"Are they digging out rock for the city?" I asked him.

"They're condemned prisoners digging their own graves,"

he said expressionlessly. "Another group will fill in the graves and dig new ones for themselves."

"That's something new," I said.

"The crime of treason has been on the rise of late."

"Numerous executions cure that quickly."

"The Derone agrees," he said.

I glanced at him. "Do you?"

"My agreement or disagreement has nothing whatsoever to do with anything."

"I see. Well I must go now to the place of prayer to offer thanks to my lord for seeing me safely across this desert. I'm sure you will excuse me."

I didn't expect that he'd actually let me go, but I thought I should make the gesture. I reached out to tap Pacesetter on the auditory surface, and Gangot leaned across to me and stayed my hand. His grip was very strong on my wrist, not that I couldn't have broken it if I'd wanted to badly enough.

"The Derone will wish to question you about your wounded friend," he said without strain.

"I scarcely knew the man," I said. "We exchanged but several words the entire night."

Gangot's eyes narrowed. "You spoke to him at length before riding off with us into the desert."

"We spoke of trivialities."

"In spite of that," the officer said, "you were still the last to speak to him. The Derone will desire an exact and thorough accounting of the conversation."

"Your own men—"

"—saw and heard nothing."

"Nothing?" I said.

"That's right."

"But they were there with him."

"You will come now," Gangot said. "The Derone is waiting."

So much for debate and discussion. Gangot released my wrist, and called out to his men. The two soldiers he'd assigned to me took their places beside me again. All the rest lined up behind us in orderly ranks of five. Then Captain Gangot led us down the dune, and across the intervening space to the city.

The city stank to high heaven. Its streets were broad and winding, filled to the brim with people. They dodged carelessly out of our way as we rode through their midst. Apparently they'd had some practice at it. We didn't run any of them down, though a few came uncomfortably close. Some of the younger ones even made a game of it, like amateur bullfighters, waiting until the last possible instant before leaping aside. We ignored them and kept on.

Tradesmen hawked their wares and argued incessantly with customers over prices. Street minstrels sang and played their instruments, the atonal chanterlike one being the most popular. Naked kids danced to the music. Ragged beggars begged, but not from us. From us they turned away. Here and there soldiers marched or swaggered, some with girls on their arms, some with burnished crossbows. It was obviously the coming weapon.

Flies buzzed, an infinitude. Scores of animals were underfoot, dogs and cats and chickens and pigs, or reasonable facsimiles of them, but no horses or cows. There were other animals that I nearly recognized. One was a sort of bald and cockeyed monkey with a distorted human skull. It clung to a woman's shoulder, peering solemnly about, tiny paws planted in her hair, its long tail curled around one of her breasts. Another creature seemed almost mythological, a breed of mutation probably, a thing between serpent and fowl. We kept on.

The noise was constant, the noise, the stink, and the flies, and the heat was stifling. Sanitation and sewage facilities were nonexistent, but the people weren't inhibited by this. They shit or shat or whatever the term is, whenever the spirit moved them, and pissed up against the sides of soap chalk buildings. Their disease rate must have been staggering. Just being there, I felt infected. Nausea and dizziness hit me. I fought it.

A young boy came running out from noplace in particular and tugged at Gangot's leg. I expected Gangot to kick the boy away, but instead he bent down, took the boy under the arms with his strong hands, and swung him into the saddle. There the boy rode proudly for about ten meters, waving and calling to people, delighted and joyful. Then Gangot dropped him off with an easy gentleness. He hadn't spoken a word to the boy, hadn't even altered his frozen expression. I wasn't sure what I should think.

We kept on, turning, turning again. The city was laid out haphazardly. Pacesetter didn't like it any more than I did. All the frenetic activity, the crowds and jostling, all of it, made him skittish, and I had to reassure him regularly. It would have been nice if someone had been there to do the same for me. My nerves were frayed to a fringe. Extreme sensory stimulation, insufficient rest and a strange diet, plus much uncertainty, equals overloaded circuits. More than anything, I wanted to be elsewhere, out of it, away from it, somewhere cool and quiet and sane. We kept on.

The streets widened in places, closed up in others. Once we were forced to go in single file, with Gangot in the lead and me next. I had to duck my head every few meters to avoid the awnings that shaded merchant stalls. Buy this, buy that, for sale, for sale. We turned and turned again. The sun beat down on us. Smoke rose from fires, hammers rang on anvils, potters' wheels spun, weavers plied their looms. Blind windows had lids of tattered cloth that flapped in the breeze. We passed a stall hung with cages, a rainbow aviary, trilling their hearts out, as though in desperate competition. Though *The Mikado* drowned out most of their songs, their plumage was vividly beautiful. But I couldn't help but picture the cage bottoms. Past experience conditions the present experience, and my attitude towards birds is relentlessly negative. Present experience is, of course, past experience for the future, but fuck all that.

We kept on, ever on. There was plenty of casual violence here, bred by the poverty, fostered by the heat, reinforced by excessive crowding. It seemed that everywhere I turned someone was into a scuffle with someone else. Twice I wanted to intervene, once with a woman and a bloody infant, once with what looked like a rape in progress. My business wasn't to intervene though. I was a kirlu, not a cop, praying for people, not policing them. The music from the sky was more real anyway, the quaint antiquated comic opera, more real than the reality, at least when I shut my eyes. But even then my nose betrayed me, betrayed me betrayal most foul.

By the time we reached the Derone's palace, I was utterly totally sick of Klask'an. And just plain sick.

We dismounted in a large open courtyard full of foot soldiers, sweating their asses off in precision parade ground march drill. I whacked Pacesetter on the snout, and told him to be good. I'd see him again soon. The multipede snorted softly, so sad that we had to part. Gangot gave orders to his men, dismissing most of them. Then he called me and the two who had witnessed the daytime landing to his side, and together he and I and they climbed up the steps of the palace. The palace was square, like everything else in the city, and much too big.

I'd seen a lot of oversized buildings before, and this one didn't impress me a bit. All my architectural impression circuits had been blown by a somewhat bigger building, further away from this one than anyone here could imagine. I mean further away than nearly anyone here could imagine. There were perhaps a few here, with a similar ticket to mine, who could imagine it easily. I would be very unwise to allow myself to forget that.

The wide flight of steps led up to a huge entranceway flanked by a pair of soldiers. They presented arms to Gangot's red plume. Their crossbows were elegant, as befitted a palace guard. The shaped metal on their multipede hide uniforms was polished gold, and broke the hot sunlight up into many brilliant beacons. Their faces might well have been chipped from anthracite, or from any other hard black substance not flesh. Flesh wouldn't maintain such rigidity.

Gangot gave them a command, and they returned to attention. We passed through the entrance and into a carpeted corridor and a taste of cool air. I was so relieved I nearly collapsed, but the sky music buoyed me up. *The flowers that bloom in the spring tra la have nothing to do with the case.* We proceeded down the corridor, and more guards were stationed at intervals. It reminded me of the BETA building back on Earth.

Brass oil lamps flickered on the walls. I noticed that on the left the lamps were held by a double set of scaly talons, like the claws of a griffin or some equally legendary beast. But on the right only a single set of talons supported the lamps. I wondered whether the artist who'd made them had died before he could get the job done, or whether the disparity had to do with a local custom my hypnocourse had missed. Our data on this planet had been a bit sketchy in some of the details, and I decided the best way to find out for sure was to ask.

"Lamp holders?" Gangot said.

"They're different on either side."

He glanced back at me. "They've always been like that."

"So odd though," I said.

Gangot stopped underneath one, gritted his teeth, and appeared to be irritated. "The difference between them is slight."

"But why any difference at all?"

"Artists are crazy." Gangot was a keen student of human nature. "And kirlus are worse, fasting in the desert, living like lizards, dreaming up visions, maddened by the sun."

"Not to mention the moons," I added helpfully.

"Let's get moving." He gestured to the witnesses, and started to walk again. "The Derone awaits."

"Yes sir," Gilbert, the first witness, said.

"Yes sir," Sullivan, the second witness, said.

And that was that for the lamps. *H.M.S. Pinafore* came on as we walked along. We took a left and there was another corridor, this one slanting downward at about a fifteen degree angle. Then things began to get confusing. Corridors branched off corridors, twisted and turned, and branched off other corridors. We went left and right, or right and left, I can't remember which. The palace was a maze. But Gangot never paused, he never hesitated. How he was able to navigate without a map I had no idea.

As we went deeper into the palace, the temperature kept going down. At its lowest it couldn't have been much over eighty. And the guards grew thicker the deeper we went. The intervals between them grew less. I thought that this duty, this marvelous refrigerated duty, must have been highly esteemed. But later I learned that it wasn't always quite so marvelous.

We were only stopped twice. Gangot spoke briefly once, and once sharply, and we were passed on through. We went this way and that, and that way and this, and all around the horn. The lamplight distorted our shadows. Desert dust billowed off my robes, settling into the dark red carpet. My bells jingled distantly. Someone was singing about *his sisters and his cousins whom he reckons up by dozens and his aunts.* I prepared myself for subvocalization.

"Peter." I paused. "Peter."

"Hi there."

"Cut the music."

"What do you want to hear instead?"

"Silence."

"You've got it."

The sudden lack of noise was weird, like a vacuum in my brain. "Now I can think."

"That's debatable."

"How is your guest doing?"

"Fine."

"Any adverse reaction?"

"He dozes a lot."

"Shock?"

"Chloral hydrate."

"Ah so," I said. "Whoops."

"Did you say whoops?"

"Something's coming up," I said. "Get off the line."

"Aye aye sir."

His transmitter clicked. We had reached a door at the end of a corridor. The door had elaborate carvings, heads of monsters, tortured humans, death and disfigurement. A single man stood by the door, dressed like a guard but without a crossbow. He held a large club with a rounded tip. Behind him was a brazen gong with a greenish tinge to it, a rough and convex surface in the lamplight that warped everything it reflected.

"Announce us," Gangot said.

"Who are you?" the guard asked.

Gangot showed annoyance. "You know who I am."

"But I don't know these others."

"They're with me."

The guard twitched his club. "Are you expected?"

"We're expected," Gangot said. "Announce us."

The guard, or doorman or whatever, nodded. He turned and struck the gong with his club, a wavering bass note that reverberated down the length of the corridor. From within, from behind the door, came an answering note, a shorter one. The guard struck his gong swiftly three times, the tones blending together into a crescendo. From within came an echo of harmony, as though three different gongs were being played. The guard nodded again.

"You may enter," he said.

"On your knees," Gangot told us.

Then he knelt down himself, and the witnesses knelt, and I followed suit. The guard remained to one side. Using the tip of his club, he pushed the door open. With Gangot in the lead, on all fours, we entered a room. I had to do my best to keep from getting tangled up in my robes, which had a sly tendency to drag me down by the neck as I crawled on them.

The door swung shut behind us. Here the carpet was colored mainly blue, with designs of many other colors woven in. I could see the designs quite clearly because my head was bowed and the lamps were bright. Gargoyles were very popular, if they were gargoyles. They may just as easily have been real animals, sports that had emerged from high radioactivity areas. Representations of women copulating with the gargoyles were also very popular. The one directly below my eyes had an unclad nubile black maiden, impaled in agony on a curved white tusk and dripping crimson threads. It was nicely portrayed, but didn't exactly arouse me, not even to disgust. I had to use most of my energy just to stay awake.

Incense was thick in the air. My peripheral vision hinted that the rest of the room was enormous, and I felt an almost kinesthetic sense of open space around me, a reverse of the feeling I'd had in the cramped corridors that had brought us here. Gangot's dusty sandals were in front of me. I could see them there less than a meter away, but I couldn't see far in focus beyond them without lifting my head, and I didn't particularly want to lift my head. His wake had left brownish streaks across the carpet, like a nasty comment on the nasty artwork. He began to chant.

"The Derone is mighty."

"The Derone is mighty," Gilbert and Sullivan responded, both of them to my left.

"The Derone is merciful," Gangot said.

"The Derone is merciful," the witnesses repeated after him, and this time I joined them.

"The Derone is wise."

"The Derone is wise."

"The Derone is just."

"The Derone is just."

"The Derone is tolerant."

"The Derone is tolerant."

Gangot summed up. "The Derone is mighty, merciful, wise, just, and tolerant." The officer stopped and then began again on a new tack. "The shells of the sea whisper his name."

"The shells of the sea whisper his name," Gilbert and Sullivan and I repeated.

"The mountains echo with his praise."

"The mountains echo with his praise."

"The sands revere his footsteps."

"The sands revere his footsteps."

"Joy to those in his favor."

"Joy to those in his favor."

"Woe to those who must know his wrath."

"Woe to those who must know his wrath."

"Truly he shall live long and prosper and his enemies shall not prevail against him or his people."

"Truly he shall live long and prosper and his enemies shall not prevail against him or his people."

"It is so."

"It is so."

We stopped chanting and waited.

Then, "Arise Captain," said an effeminate, but authoritative, tenor voice. "All of you may rise."

"Thank you Derone," Gangot said as we rose.

"Thank you Derone," we echoed, our eyes cast down.

The effeminate voice said, "I hear that yet another star fell in the desert and returned to the sky."

"Yes Derone," Gangot said.

"Tell me everything you know about it."

"Hey Meas," Peter said.

I sighed. "Yeah?"

"Soraft says to watch out for that guy, he isn't nearly as sweet as his litany."

"He isn't?" I subvocalized.

"Nope."

"I'm disillusioned."

Gangot had launched into an unadorned account of the second star fall, and of what he knew of my part in it and that of the unhappy witnesses. I'd been standing with my head bowed, and now I glanced up to survey the room. My peripheral vision hadn't failed me. The room was enormous. It was filled to overflowing with guards, all of whom were armed and looked dangerous. A lot of statues were also scattered about, most of them done in the popular sex death horror mode. Heavy tapestries hung on the walls, their fabric designed in a similar fashion.

The Derone was straight ahead, reclining on a divan. He was in his late twenties, by my estimate, bearded and grossly fat. To either side of him was an attendant in brown waving a fan with vigor. The Derone's silken blue toga rippled in the breezes. He was surrounded by naked women, one of whom had his cock out. She kissed it and licked it, crooned to it softly, caressed it, her face entranced, apparently mesmerized by it. The rest of the women were beautiful, and were placed to be within easy reach. The Derone reached for them often.

Behind him stood a somber attendant in black, holding a golden goblet with a filigree pattern. Further away to one side was an ancient wizened old man, seated on a huge stone chair with a blanket over his legs. I presumed that the blanket was all that kept him warm in that chilling eighty degree frost. A number of tables were set up for easy access, heaped with delicacies, with fruits and nuts and meats and wines. The Derone ate an apple while the girl was ministering to him.

Gangot continued with his unadorned account, and I discovered the purpose of the goblet. The Derone made a sign with his apple core to the attendant in black. The attendant came quickly and quietly forward and knelt beside the divan. When the Derone made another sign, this time a convulsive one, the attendant tilted the goblet, tilted it so as to be a receptacle. Now the girl's hand was rhythmically pumping the cock, and at the climactic burst, the goblet caught the seed of the royal ejaculation. The flow was a prodigious one, and she squeezed out every drop.

Then the attendant rose and carried the goblet to the old man. The old man took it and drank, his head thrown back, the muscles working in his wattled neck. This was a bit of ritual that hadn't been mentioned in any of the intelligence reports I'd studied back at BETA. But then a lot of other things had been left out as well. It was a wonder I'd been given the file on the right planet, let alone expect it to be anywhere near complete.

The attendant took back the empty goblet, and carefully ran a cloth around inside. He showed the clean goblet to the old man, received a nod, passed the old man the cloth, and went back to his station by the divan. Gangot finished the account. The old man slid the cloth under his blanket and spoke in an effeminate tenor voice. That stopped me for a beat, until I realized my mistake. The Derone wasn't the young man as I'd assumed. He was the old man. The young man was apparently some kind of pleasure proxy, used by the old man vicariously and voyeuristically as a surrogate. The old man requested the witnesses to tell him what they had seen in the desert.

"Toraq," Gangot said.

Sullivan stepped forward, fearful and hesitant, head hung down, not bowed, and said pathetically, "Derone forgive me. My courage fled when the star fell. I buried my face in the sand and didn't see anything until the star was gone." He stood there, silent now, and trembled.

"Your courage fled you?"

"Yes Derone." Sullivan stared at the carpet.

"You buried your face in the sand?"

"Yes Derone."

"Look at me," the old man snapped.

Sullivan raised his head. "Yes Derone."

"Do you know the price of cowardice?"

"Yes Derone." Sullivan's voice was weak.

"What is it?"

Sullivan whispered, "Death."

"Louder coward."

"Death."

"Lieutenant Groll," the old man said.

A taller soldier detached himself from the retinue and presented arms to the old man. "My Derone."

"Kill him."

There was a measure of enjoyment in the words. Lieutenant Groll pivoted smartly, brought his crossbow into position, and put a bolt into Sullivan's chest. The soldier collapsed on the carpet. Gangot squatted, checked him, and nodded, expressionless. The Derone was smiling. I felt certain he hoped that Gilbert would do no better than Sullivan had. The Derone's pleasure proxy, if that's what he was, was lying back now, eyes half shut, idly stroking the nearby female flesh. He was no doubt storing up energy. The old man made a gesture, and Sullivan was removed. Lieutenant Groll went back to his place with the retinue.

"Let the second soldier speak," the old man said.

"Meskaw," Gangot said.

Gilbert stepped forward shakily. "My Derone."

"I trust your observations will be more useful to us." The old man was still smiling wolfishly.

"Yes Derone." Gilbert paused. "I uh I uh—"

"Get on with it."

Gilbert plunged. "I was close to the star when it fell. It was bright and silvery, larger than this room, and it twinkled like a candle. A hand of silvery fire reached out to where the wounded drover lay and picked him up. The hand took him away to the heart of the star, after which he was lost to my sight in the brightness. In another instant the star was gone, risen once more to the sky." Gilbert let out his breath with a hiss.

"The star twinkled?" the old man said.

"Yes Derone."

"And a hand of, what was it?"

"Fire," Gilbert said.

"Silvery fire?"

"Yes Derone."

"A hand of silvery fire picked up the drover?" The old man was being very serious now.

"Yes Derone."

The old man pursed his lips shrewdly. "The drover didn't by any chance burn when this hand of flame touched him?"

"No Derone." But Gilbert sounded trapped.

"He didn't burn at all?"

"No Derone."

"Did he singe a little perhaps?"

Gilbert swallowed audibly. "No Derone."

"How fortunate for him," the old man said. "But how unfortunate for you. That other was bad enough with his unsoldierly fears, but worse by far is one who would lie to his ruler."

"No Derone, no oh no." Gilbert prostrated himself on the carpet. "I couldn't lie to you."

The old man's smile returned. "Then possibly you went to sleep while all of this was going on. And possibly what you have told me was only a vivid dream. Could that be the excuse for your moronic fabrication?"

"My Derone," Gilbert moaned.

"There is no excuse," the old man said.

Gilbert groveled in abject terror. "I beseech you—"

"Be silent." The old man's gaze shifted, resting on me briefly, and then moving on. "Captain Gangot."

"Yes Derone," Gangot said.

"We must show this one exactly what the effect a hand of fire can have on the human body." The old man considered for a moment. "Construct the hand of iron, and bind him to the palm, and heat it up slowly. The longer he lives the better the lesson will be, and the greater will be your reward for teaching him. But take care not to allow him to die too soon, nor to ease the torture unnecessarily in the prolonging of it. I intent to be there to watch it personally."

"Yes Derone," Gangot said with no visible emotion. "Arrangements will be made to forge the hand at once."

"That's fine," the old man said. "Lieutenant Groll."

The officer presented arms. "My Derone."

"Take him out." The old man pointed to the quivering creature on the carpet. "Lock him up."

"Yes Derone."

"Give him plenty of water," the old man added. "Just water, no food. He should sweat profusely on the hand, and he'll need some moisture to spare."

"Yes Derone."

Lieutenant Groll spoke to a pair of the guards. They took the prostrated soldier by the legs, and simply hauled him out, leaving him without a trace of hope or dignity. Groll went back to his place again. The old man's gaze returned to me, and this time I felt the chill. It came from within him, exiting through the eyes, like stalactite shards of ice.

I hated him, despised him. The bastard was cruel and capricious and arbitrary. He was also very intelligent, the lousy son of a bitch. This meant that I had to beware of him, and hold my tongue, and not let my hatred become defiance. I would have to be like that pleasure proxy, which is to say, I had to be whatever the old man wanted me to be. At the same time I had to make him want what I wanted him to want. I stepped forward.

"So you were the drover's companion," he said.

I shook my head. "No Derone."

"You weren't?" The old man favored Captain Gangot with a frown. "Was I misinformed?"

"No Derone," Gangot said. "The kirlu and the drover were together when we found them."

"Were you?" the old man asked me.

"Yes Derone."

"That is contradictory." The old man plucked at the blanket in his lap. "You were with him?"

"Yes Derone."

"But you weren't companions?"

I shrugged. "Only in the most approximate sense."

"The kirlu was tending the drover's wound," Gangot said drily. "I call that more proximate than not."

"So do I," the old man said. "Well kirlu?"

"I spent but a single night with him," I said. "Before then we were total strangers. Yet it wasn't until a short while ago that I understood who he was."

The old man cocked his head. "Who was he?"

"An agent of my lord."

"Your lord deity?"

"Yes Derone," I said.

"Which deity?"

"Ytrifg the Inscrutable One."

"And the drover was his agent?" the old man said with a faintly comic air of getting things straight.

"Yes Derone."

"How did you determine this?"

I scuffed my sandal against the carpet. "Clearly the drover was not a drover at all. Ytrifg sent him to test the extent of my zeal and fortitude. I can see that now."

"Explain his method of testing you." The old bastard seemed to be fascinated, which of course was the whole idea.

"He professed to be a disbeliever," I said, "and he questioned me on matters of faith."

"What did he ask you?"

"I'm not certain that I remember exactly."

"You had better remember," the old man said. "This is an affair of the utmost importance."

"I am well aware of that." My gaze drifted piously heavenward. "Everything my lord does is of the utmost importance." There were some fantastic designs on the ceiling.

"Come come kirlu."

"I don't wish to make a mistake," I said.

"Making me wait too long would be a mistake." The old man leaned towards me, on the edge of his big stone chair, his blanket twisted in his fingers.

"My recollection is imprecise."

"Do your best," the old man said. "But do it."

I nodded. "He asked me if I truly felt my lord was responsible for the star that fell in the desert that night. I told him that I truly did feel this. He asked me then if I didn't feel it may have had some other cause or origin. I told him no, that couldn't be. A natural star cannot go back to the sky after it has fallen to the ground. He suggested that it might not have been a star."

"What else would it be?" the old man said anxiously. "Did he suggest an alternative?"

I shook my head. "No Derone."

"Did he ask you anything further?"

"No Derone," I said. "He came and tested me and found me strong in my faith. Then Ytrifg took him home."

"He was wounded."

"Yes Derone."

The old man leaned back in his chair. "Were you present when he received the wound?"

"Yes Derone."

"How did he get it?"

"This happened at night," I said, "near the drovers' campsite. A gang of bandits attacked in an effort to steal away part of the herd. He fought against them alongside the drovers, which is why I thought that he was a drover too."

"A logical conclusion to draw," the old man said. "He must have been trying to ingratiate himself."

"In the course of the battle in the dark," I went on, "a bandit chopped off his hand with a sword. He was hurt very badly, and wasn't able to leave with the rest. I stayed behind to care for him, though there was really little that I could do."

"You and one other stayed behind," the old man said. "Who was the other who stayed behind with you?"

I shrugged. "A friend of his."

"You're sure they were friends?"

"They acted like friends," I said.

The old man worked his way through it out loud. "The one was hurt, the other was killed. And that was why the one was picked up. Because he was badly wounded, he needed special attention, and because the other was dead." The old man turned to Gangot. "He may be back again, the one who survived. Would you know him if you saw him?"

"No Derone," Gangot said. "I paid him no heed."

The old man scowled. "You should have. A good officer is an alert officer. Five lashes to impress that on you."

"Yes Derone." Gangot had the emotionless tone of voice down pat. "Five lashes."

"We have to be ready for him," the old man said. "Tell your soldiers to be on the watch for a one handed drover."

"There must be hundreds," Gangot said, "perhaps more, in the city, missing one hand. It's a common injury."

"Which hand was it?" the old man asked me.

"The right."

"That narrows it down," the old man said. "The wound would be recent. That narrows it further. But don't ignore anyone with what appears to be a wound that has healed." The old man turned to me. "Can you describe him?"

"Yes Derone," I said. "He's tall. His teeth stick out slightly, and show when his face is relaxed. He has a large hairy birthmark above his left eyebrow. The top of his left ear is missing. He twitches the corner of his mouth when he talks."

"You hear, Captain?" the old man said. "This is a kirlu who looks at things. What's your name?" he asked me.

"Gnarla," I said. "But I don't understand. Who do you think my patron's agent is?"

"Never mind," the old man said. "You spoke to him before you rode into the desert with my troops."

"Yes Derone."

"You spoke of what?"

"Nothing consequential."

The old man flapped his blanket most impatiently. "You let me be the judge of that."

"Well uh uh uh—" I broke down.

"Are you afraid of me?" the old man asked.

"Yes Derone."

"No need to be."

"But I am," I said. "Your magnificence is overwhelming, and your radiance dims the sun."

He sat up straighter. "Of course, of course."

"My limbs are trembling."

"Of course they are." Abruptly his tone became gentle. "There there kirlu. Be frank and open with me. I won't harm you. You spoke to the drover of what?"

"He wasn't a drover," I said.

"Now kirlu."

The time was ripe for me to make my move. "I told him I had a premonition that we wouldn't be together again. I thought it was because he would die of his wound before I could get back to him. As it happened, I was correct, though not completely. Ytrifg took him. He didn't die of his wound, but I was correct about, about our not being together again. Often I have such premonitions. I can sometimes see the future plainly."

The old man raised his eyebrow. "Can you?"

"Yes Derone."

"An interesting talent." He frowned. "Can you read my future too?"

I met his chilly eyes. "Yes Derone."

"Read it then."

"You will conquer the world," I said. "There are forces acting on your behalf that cannot be quelled."

The old man looked at me cunningly. "So that is my future as you read it with your talent?"

"Yes Derone."

"Can you read your own future?" he said.

"I can a little."

"Read it for me, and for yourself."

"I see that I will remain with you," the move of moves, "and assist you in your many conquests."

"And so you shall," he said.

"Thank Ytrifg."

The old man made a gesture towards the pleasure proxy's naked women. "Zorane."

"My Derone," said one of the women.

"Bring this kirlu to a room of joy, and do whatever he bids you there." To me he said, "You will find that I am very generous in rewarding faithful service. Be as faithful to your new master as you are to your lord. But be less than faithful and you will swiftly feel my wrath."

I went to my knees. "I wish no rewards, I wish only to serve. To serve is reward enough."

"Captain Gangot," the old man said.

"My Derone."

"You may take your five lashes when your soldier sits on the hand of iron."

"Yes Derone."

"You may go now."

Gangot dropped to his knees, then stood up and bowed, and still bowing, backed his way out the door. Three gongs, the inside did have three, rang him out. The old man dismissed me also, telling me to remain beyond the door. Then he asked the girl to stay with him for a moment before leading me to my room. I got to my feet and bowed out, wondering what he had to say to her. He was clever, for all his meanness, the bastard. I resolved to continue to be even more so.

The guard outside the door stared at me suspiciously. I stared back until he looked away. Gangot was waiting for me, a few steps down the corridor. He beckoned to me to join him. I went over to where he stood. He walked with me a few more steps down the corridor, and the guard stared at both of us with equal suspicion, hefting his club almost as though he intended to use it. Gangot came up close to my side.

"You appear to be a visionary," he said softly.

"Perhaps I am."

"A visionary must watch what he sees."

"Is that a warning?" I said.

"Perhaps it is."

He started to leave, but I detained him. "You don't seem to care too much for your men."

"I don't?"

"One of them dies and the other one fries."

His jaw muscles tightened. "Toraq died like your acquaintance in the desert. Nothing could be done for him. The quarrel flew and that was that. There was nothing to be done."

"You could have taken his part," I said.

"There was nothing to be done."

"Not for him or for the one who's to be cooked."

"The Derone is old," Gangot said in a harsh whisper. "He nears his death. It will take us a while to forge the hand of iron. The Derone may be dead before then. The Derone's successor whom you saw by his side, is slothful and useless but not vicious. He only wants his fleshy delights, and won't pursue the matter."

"The old man may live for years."

Gangot faced me squarely. "You're the prophet with the vision of the future. Will the old man live for years or not?"

"Some things are closed to me." I was a prophet without honor. "He may live, he may not."

"In case he does," Gangot said, "Meskaw will be allowed to kill himself, so at least he'll be spared the anguish of torture. The Derone will be displeased. But it will be done in such a way that he will be unable to fix the blame."

"I see," I said.

"You repeat this to him," Gangot went on, "and I'll call you a liar. The Derone will believe me. He knows that I'm loyal to him."

"But not as loyal as you are to your men."

"I assure you," he said. "I am loyal to both. My life depends on it. Do not attempt to test the matter."

I touched his shoulder. "You needn't worry."

"I'm not worried," he said. "But if I were you, I'd be most cautious. The Derone is not a person to be taken lightly. I wouldn't say a word against him myself, but he's a man who gets a very special sort of satisfaction from inflicting pain. And his whims are impossible to anticipate, even for someone who has your unusual abilities."

"All right," I said. "I won't—"

He turned to go. "That's wise." He walked away.

"Are you alone?"

I glanced at the door guard, who was distant enough, though still suspicious, and subvocalized, "More or less."

"Captain Gangot's a strange one."

"Yeah."

"Almost as strange as you."

"As me?"

"The play you just made."

"With Gangot you mean?"

"I mean becoming the palace oracle."

"Did I do it wrong?"

"It's not what you're there for. You're supposed to be there to find out why our contact went astray."

"This new position gives me more scope."

"More scope to fuck yourself up. You hang around too close to the fire, you're bound to get your ass burned off."

"Like on the hand of iron?"

"For instance."

"I'll politely decline to be seated."

"Make a break instead, as soon as you can."

"I appreciate the advice and so forth, but would you do me a small favor?"

"What?"

"Save it."

Peter made a disgusted noise, *"acchh,"* like he was spitting out my brain cells.

"How's Soraft?" I asked to change the subject.

"Up and about between naps. His wound is beginning to heal very nicely. The danger of infection is past."

"I'm glad."

"I gave him a quick hypnocourse in Basic so he wouldn't feel left out of the conversation. The course included reading skills, to give him access to our library. We've been discussing the situation down there. He isn't completely certain he wants to be hunted through the city streets. Would you like to soothe away his qualms for him?"

"Sure."

Soraft's voice had a sardonic note to it. *"Your description of me was extremely inaccurate."*

"I have a poor memory for detail."

"They'll never find me with that kind of help."

"Probably not."

"You ought to be more—"

"Someone's coming," I said. "Call me later."

To the bombilating sound of gongs, the girl backed into sight. Her behind was designed to dampen the palms, bowed over and shapely and bare. The look the door guard gave her could have hardly been classed as suspicious. She stood up straight and glanced around until she saw me. The door guard gave me a glare of pure malice. The girl joined me, smiling widely, told me she was mine, and took my arm.

We traveled down still more corridors infested by still more guards. They all still seemed alike, the guards and the corridors both. The former all seemed to know the girl, and we weren't stopped even once. Halfway down one of these endless corridors was a room with a door, defended by the usual grim soldier with the usual elegant crossbow. We paused in the lamplight for a moment, and the girl and the soldier conferred.

Apparently they'd run out of claws entirely by the time they'd got to this room. The lamp by the door was held in place only by a simple iron shelf. Somehow this made me feel a little deprived. The soldier softened enough to the girl to let us pass through the door. Inside the room was the most conspicuous bed I'd even seen in my life. I flung myself down on it, my seven bells jingling, and dust settled about me in clouds. Sleep came instantly. I don't know what the hell happened to the naked girl.

"Reveille reveille reveille, time to get up."
"Jesus Christ," I said.
"Are you up?"
"Give me a break."
"Get up."
"Wow."
I opened my eyes. They were crusted with sand. I rubbed at them and checked out the room. There were lamps, but no windows. It could have been day or night outside, not that I cared one way or the other. I was alone and groggy. My head was stuffed with bellybutton lint, and this palace no longer seemed temperate. The heat had my robes all soaked through with sweat. There was a hollow dark wet outline of my body on the blue cotton sheet of the featherbed.

"You've been asleep for fourteen hours."

"Good for me."

"You ought to be ashamed."

"Like hell I ought."

"Start moving around, pretend you're alive."

"Bullshit."

"You snore like a steam locomotive."

"Nobody made you listen."

"Now Meas."

"Why'd you wake me?"

"Soraft wants to have a talk."

"Can't it wait?"

"I don't think so."

"You wouldn't." I sighed. "Put him on."

"Gnarla?" Soraft said. *"Or Meas?"*

"It doesn't matter."

"Gnarla is my friend. Meas is a stranger to me. It does matter. I have to know which one you are."

"Maybe I'm something in between."

"There is nothing in between but an enemy."

I tried to recall what he looked like and found that I couldn't, only the grin he had flashed me when the bandits attacked us. "You have to decide on your own what I am."

"Young Peter has shown me things that twist my mind. Today he told me that soon I will have a new hand, that soon I will be whole and complete the way I was before. This seems impossible, but I believe him. He makes belief in the impossible a necessity."

"You'll have the new hand," Peter said, *"when your tissues are ready for regeneration."*

"Like a clarow regrows lost limbs."

"Pretty much."

"My heart is certain," Soraft said in a passionate tone, *"that this is magic."*

"It's just technology."

"My heart doesn't know the difference."

"Hey you guys up there," I said testily. "Could you maybe delay your discussion till later?"

. .*"Meas is in a mood,"* Peter said. *"We'd better humor him."*

Soraft said, *"The boy has told me why you are here.*

He has told me who you oppose, and what it is they are after. It sounds like some sort of a complicated game, and the reason for playing it is beyond me. You must understand, to me my world is very small, and not always kind. But—"
He ground to a halt.

"Go on," I prompted.

"My world should not be a prize in somebody's game."

"This isn't any game," I said soberly. "Now I could say that you have no choice but to do what we ask. There's no limit to what we can do to you, from growing you a new hand to enslaving your free will. I could say that you have no choice, and might as well give in to us. But I wouldn't say that. Instead I'll ask you to wait, and to trust us, if you feel you can. If you feel you can't trust us, you can return to your people. Whichever you prefer."

He paused, then said, *"I owe you my life."*

"We're even on that."

"How can we be?"

"We are."

"You want me to be sure the choice is mine."

"The choice is yours."

There was another pause, and then he said, *"I will wait,"* and I knew that would be the final word from him.

"Right," I said. "Peter."

"I'm here."

"Do you want anything else from me?"

"No I guess not."

"Then put on some string quartets."

"String quartets?"

"Yeah."

"What a drag."

"Will you put them on?"

"I will but I won't listen to them."

"Do that."

In a moment the music swelled through my brain. I counted up to ten, got out of bed, crossed the room to the door, and pushed the door open. It swung both ways, on multipede hide hinges. A guard was still stationed outside in the corridor. He may or may not have been the same guard as before.

I told him I was awake, and he grunted at me. So I let the door close between us again, and went back to the bed and sat down. Now like Soraft all I could do was wait, but at least he had Peter for company. I only had disagreeable thoughts, disagreeable thoughts and string quartets. What a drag.

Someone brought me food and left. I ate voraciously, meat in a gravy sauce, green vegetables. The time went by slowly. I used the chamber pot in the corner, a brass affair. I stretched out on the bed. The heat was not conducive to ambition. A new someone came to clear away the plates, and the chamber pot. Time continued to go by slowly. The chamber pot was replaced. Naked women took care of all the chores, and expressed a willingness to do more. But my own willingness was at too low an ebb for me to take advantage of theirs. I was tense and worried and wondering what would come next and when it would come. I had no idea how much time had passed at any given moment. My time sense is just as screwed up as my sense of direction. Some people seem to have clocks built into their skulls, and some always seem able to find their way home. I'm not one of them. I figure I'm doing fine when I can deduce which way is up and which is down. The constant flickering light of the wall lamps had a hypnotic effect on me, and I meditated on the flames and tried not to think about anything. Fire is the key to man's mastery, the servant to man's destiny, but also a servant unto itself. It is the creator and the destroyer, the true prime mover, the tongue of tongues, and its fiercest voice, its ultimate voice, resides at the divisible core of the atom. I heard it speak out once in that great loud voice, speak its most shattering thunderous and terrible statement, and that was by far the worst sound I have ever heard. But that was very bad to think about, and so I quit staring at the lamps. The heat was a scourge. My robes were sodden. I had a headache and I stank. The bellybutton lint of before had turned into frayed steel wool, and the stale specific gravity of my sweat was too heavy to lift. Time was passing slower and slower with no end in sight, not even the nice curving end of a naked palace nymph. I was all alone. The string quartets were no help. I felt as though I'd spent the better part of my life on the bed in this room. The dark wet hollow my body pressed into the mattress was as distinctive as a fingerprint. Every line and indentation of me left a mark. This tiny room felt more and more like a trap. The lack of windows was bothering me quite a bit by now, and I desperately wanted to see the sun or moons trace their paths across the sky, to see some kind of celestial motion to prove to myself that the universe was still in gear. I shut my eyes and massaged them hard, and then inside the lids I saw, with a measure of relief, whirling stars and writhing comet tails, my own little universe within. And finally I fell asleep again, and dreamed of nothing at all.

When I awoke my robes were gone and a naked girl was washing me with warm cloths and scented soap. I'd never seen the girl before, but the bath was marvelous. It was also one of the reasons why an agent isn't supposed to carry any visible equipment around with him on this sort of field trip. One can't be sure one won't be searched, either by accident or by design.

The chatter between me and the ship was all being done on a tight beam. Anything used to interrupt or locate the beam would register on the ship's security scanning devices and be misdirected by about ten kilometers. Whoever tried to track or tap on the beam would get nothing for his trouble but a wild goose chase and a hatful of meaningless static. Of course there were lots of detection devices our adversaries could use to find the stuff I had stashed inside my body. But if they knew enough to use them to search me there the deal was blown anyway.

I was beginning to feel rather clean. The girl who was bathing me was beautiful, a slender black shadow in the lamplight. I lay on my back and watched her as she worked. She seemed to be concentrating on a certain centrally situated portion of my anatomy. After a while I started to take a special interest, and I couldn't keep that interest from showing. The girl glanced up and smiled at me.

"You're awake," she said.

I smiled back. "It appears that I am."

"Are you hungry?"

"Not very," I said.

She nodded, "My name is Besaca."

"Mine is Gnarla."

"I was told you're a kirlu," she said.

"That's true."

"And also a prophet."

"I do have visions," I said.

She stroked me in such a manner as to keep my interest up. "When I was but a child I was brought to the palace to learn the ways of love. I have learned many things, and I can please you."

"I'm sure that you can."

"May I?" she said.

I hesitated. "My lord might disapprove."

"But will he?" She stroked and stroked.

"I don't know," I said with my cock pulsating spasmodically in her hand. "He's inscrutable."

She giggled. "You aren't though."

"Ummmm."

"Will you have me," she said.

I looked at her face, which was gay and expectant, and I reached out to her. "Yes."

"What about your lord?"

"He'll have to find his own woman," I said.

My period of abstinence ended there. It had been a long while, a period of sorrow, of pain and then numbness, of detention camps, of bureaucrats and desert dust, of disagreeable thoughts and string quartets. The period had lasted a long while, not as reckoned by the clock, but as reckoned by lack of desire. It had lasted for too long a while.

Besaca was most accomplished. She required quite little of me, which was really just as well. Excessive sleep tends to make me sluggish, and I felt a bit uneasy and out of practice. But she was active and confident enough for the both of us. She encouraged me and took me into the midst of her, all strength and warmth and sweet sharp fragrances. Afterwards we lay side by side.

"You're very gentle," she said.

I turned to her. "So are you."

"Did I give you pleasure?"

"Much," I said.

She smiled. "I'm glad."

"My what a jolly occasion," Peter said joltingly. *"Too bad you haven't got a televisor unit with you too."*

"You fucking peeping tom," I subvocalized.

"Now that's no attitude to take. I'm not a peeping tom. That's the problem. I can't see a thing."

"Go away."

"I merely want to further my education."

Besaca patted my shoulder. "I have something for you."

"Something more?" I said.

"I'm listening closely."

"Shut the fuck up," I subvocalized.

"All the better to hear you."

Besaca had gotten out of bed, plucked a bright scrap of cloth from the floor, and was holding it out. "To replace your robes."

It was a red and gold toga, made of silk, or of something similar to silk. I got up and Besaca helped me to put it on. I raised my arms and let it settle down over me like a gossamer tent. The material was smooth and comfortable. It reached to just below my knees and left my arms completely bare.

"Nice," I said.

"Do you like it?"

"I do."

"It fits you well," Besaca said happily. "And by its colors the guards will know that you may pass freely within the palace."

"There's just one thing."

"What?"

"How do you find your way around in here?" I said.

"You unroll a thread behind you, and then you follow it back," Peter said, just to needle me, no doubt.

Besaca gestured gracefully, small breasts bobbing. "There are corridors of no importance. They can be recognized by the blank shelves that hold the wall lamps in place. There is one major corridor. It leads from the outside to the main chamber. Along it each lamp is held by sets of golog claws."

"I see," I said.

"Crazy artists indeed."

"When you are going towards the main chamber," Besaca went on, there will be a double set of claws to your left. When you are going away from the chamber, towards the outside, the double set will be on your right, and the single set will be on your left. Only this corridor with the single set means anything. The others all either lead into it, or they lead to dead ends."

"Another mystery solved."

I said, "I can come and go freely?"

"As freely as you wish."

"Where are we now?"

"Physically or philosophically?"

"This is the Room of Joy," she said, "in the Hall of the Dancing Green Autruth. Anyone among the guards in the palace can tell you how to return here."

"Unrolling a thread is more fun."

"Excuse me," I said to the girl, and got up and went over to the chamber pot, and lifted my toga hem. "Peter."

"Hi there."

I began to piss into the pot. "Why is it that you feel such a tremendous need to annoy me?"

"I haven't got anything better to do."

"Annoy Soraft."

"I can't, he's asleep."

"Wake him up the way you woke me up."

"He'd hit me."

"Now listen."

"Uh huh."

"I want you to stop with all the wisecracks."

"You're a party pooper."

"Will you stop?"

"I'll try."

"But will you stop?"

"I refuse to make promises I'm not sure I can keep."

"Peter."

"I'll try."

"Try really hard." I'd run out of piss. "God will reward you." I shook off the last few drops, and went back to the girl. "I want to speak with Captain Gangot. Do you know who he is?"

She nodded. "Yes."

"Do you know where I might find him?"

"At this time of day he's probably with his men, out drilling in the field behind the palace."

"I bet he does that a lot," I said.

And then I reached out and took Besaca into my arms again, and went about furthering Peter's education some more, and while I was at it I furthered my own a bit too.

I was blinded by the sunlight outside the palace, and the heat was murder in the hundred and tenth degree. But the air had a nice fresh salty taste that blew in off the ocean. And my new silken toga was a distinct improvement over my robes, though I sort of missed the protection of my knots and bells. Peter had put something on which was mellow and tuneful and mildly jazzy, and which was a distinct improvement over the string quartets.

Eventually my eyes adjusted to the brightness. As I rounded a corner of the palace, the first thing I saw was a target range. The range had been set up along one of the palace walls, and a group of soldiers was using it to perfect their crossbowmanship. They were pretty deadly, from what I could see, to everything but the targets. I gave them a wide berth.

Beyond them was the field, a level grassy square that covered about four acres, bounded by rows of planted trees, and by the city and the palace. The field may have been neat once. It may have been landscaped to give the palace a pleasant view, and to provide a decent place for the Royal cookouts and festivals. But now it was badly torn up.

Out in the middle of it a squad of men was engaged in close order drill on the backs of multipedes. I shaded my eyes with a hand, and watched them for a while. They were mounted well and I was suitably impressed with them. Woe betide anyone who got in their path. The deplorable state of the field was an indicator of what would happen to anyone who did.

Another squad was naked and gleaming, and I felt sorry for them. They shone with perspiration as they grunted their way through a series of rugged calisthenics. At the far end of the field, to my left, a mock battle was being fought. Teams of soldiers were going up against each other with swords and shields. The noise of them clashing was clearly audible from where I stood.

All in all they didn't look much like a peacetime army, but sometimes it's hard to tell. Maybe they were just there to act as some sort of a deterrent. And maybe shit would change to gold and put all moneylenders out of business. After I'd watched for about twenty minutes, an officer with a red plume in his helmet rode by. I flagged him down.

"Is Captain Gangot out here somewhere?" I said.

The officer turned in his saddle and pointed towards the mounted men. "He's over there."

"Would you mind asking him to join me?"

"I have other things to do," the officer said disdainfully, "than to run errands for civilians."

With a maximum of humble dignity I said, "I am Gnarla the kirlu, the Derone's new seer."

"I'll tell Captain Gangot you want him," the officer said in a very sour key, and wheeled his multipede about, and rode out across the field.

"Sir request permission to speak sir," Peter said in a curt cadet voice that cut through the mellow tuneful jazzy music.

"Be brief," I said.

"Sir what's Gangot on call for sir?"

"Quit stirring me."

"Sir are you certain sir?"

"Knock it off."

"I really wouldn't like for you to feel that I'm lacking in proper respect for you."

"Come on come on."

"What's Gangot on call for?"

"I want him to help me track down our missing link."

"Mr. Atherton."

"Right."

"Do you think you'll find him?"

"I might."

"And if you don't?"

"I don't."

"You sound disgusted."

"Only because I am."

"But you know something?"

"Hummm."

"In a way I envy you."

"Why's that?"

"All the fresh air and healthful exercise you're getting. Not to mention the indoor fringe benefits. You should be paying CROWN, not the other way around. The rumors have it, by the by, you're being paid lots. Is that true?"

"More or less."

"How much?"

"I swore I'd never say."

"Just a hint."

"Nope an oath is an oath."

There was a pause, and then he said, *"Whatever the amount is the rumors also have it that they aren't actually expecting you to live long enough to collect."*

"Rumors from where?"

"The usual informed sources."

"They expect me to get killed on this job."

"So I hear."

"I hope I fool them."

"Good luck."

I glanced across the field. "Gangot's coming now."

"And you want me to shut up."

"I'd appreciate it."

"Will you love me forever if I do?"

"Probably not."

"I'll shut up anyway."

"Terrific," I said.

The music swelled, still mellow, still tuneful, still jazzy. Gangot approached at a canter, rigidly straight in his saddle, a fine example for the troops. I remained in one spot, waiting for him to arrive. The sun was still murder. He pulled to a stop in front of me, and dismounted from his multipede.

"You're dressed well today," he said.

I shrugged. "My clothes are unimportant. This is what I was given to wear. I have two things to ask of you."

"Ask."

"Firstly I'd like my clarow back," I said "The animal was a gift from my parents and I'd hate to lose him."

Gangot nodded. "He's been kept in our stables for you. You can have him whenever you like. What's the second thing?"

"The use of one of your spare soldiers as a bodyguard and as a guide to the city."

"You need a bodyguard?" Gangot said.

I stared at the ground, then stooped, and picked up a clover. "I feel insecure."

"You do?"

"A common feeling."

Gangot's eyebrows rose. "But perhaps less common is a fortune teller who feels insecure about the future."

"My fortune telling comes and goes intermittently," I said. "My insecurity is with me all the time."

"A shame," Gangot said with no expression.

I spun the clover away by the stem like a miniature toystore top. "The worst thing about the future is that it can't be avoided."

"But people do try to avoid it."

"And none of them succeeds." I rested my case. "None of them, especially me."

Gangot delivered the summation. "So everyone is insecure, the fortune tellers more than most. That makes sense of a sort. You also need a guide to the city?"

"There are parts of Klask'an," I said, "that I haven't seen yet, that I've always wanted to see."

"Which parts?"

"Those that dislike having kirlus about."

"For instance?" Gangot said.

"The wine district."

Gangot considered for a moment. "I can let you have

Nylad for the afternoon. He's strong enough to protect you, he'll enjoy a day off, and he's familiar with the wineshops."

"Thank you," I said.

"You'd best keep him out of the wineshops however, or he'll be the one you'll need the protection from."

"I'll do that."

"Anything else?" Gangot said.

"That man of yours, the one who lied and was sentenced to death by torture, how is he?"

"Dead."

I frowned. "By torture?"

"By poison," Gangot said tonelessly.

"You missed your chance at a big reward."

"There'll be other chances."

I said, "Did the man die quickly?"

"Yes he did."

"Was the Derone disappointed?"

"Very disappointed," Gangot said.

"That's too bad."

Gangot used a stirrup to swing aboard his multipede, and took up the slack on the reins. "Apparently someone helped the man to die. The Derone has ordered a full investigation of the incident and has placed me in charge."

"Ah," I said.

"He has me do much of his investigating."

I grinned. "Better not let this culprit escape the way you did the one out in the desert."

"The traitor will be caught," Gangot said firmly.

"I pity him."

Gangot leaned forward to tap his multipede on the auditory area. "Nylad will be along shortly with your clarow."

"Thanks again," I said.

"My pleasure." Gangot turned his mount and rode off stiffly across the field, his red plume fluttering from his helmet.

"Is he gone?"

"He's gone."

"The way that guy talks, can he see through your disguise, or am I just being paranoid?"

"You're just being paranoid."

"He definitely doesn't believe you're an oracle."

"I know."

"Don't you care?"

"Sure I'm all broken up about it."

"You don't care."

"No I guess I don't."

"Well if you don't care I don't care either."

"We've finally agreed on something."

"Hey you're right. This is an historic occasion. We ought to celebrate. I'm going to have me a strawberry malted. I'd offer you one too, but there's no way I can—"

"Peter."

"You want me to shut up."

"Would you?"

"Glad to oblige."

He shut up and put on another lousy goddam string quartet, and I stood in the hot noonday sun and I suffered, and no longer felt a bit sorry for the sweltering troops out there.

Pacesetter had been outfitted with a saddle. It didn't seem to bother him any, assuming he even noticed he had it on. When Nylad led him over to where I was waiting, the multipede gave out a loud squeal, and trotted the last couple of meters and into my open arms. I got up off the ground and clouted him across the snout with my fist. Then he washed me down with his tongue, and I put my arm in his mouth. After that we got going.

My guide and bodyguard was a jovial bruiser with no teeth and an unlimited quantity of scar tissue. He had a vocabulary of six or seven words, and all of them were unintelligible. We threaded our way through the streets in relative silence, while the noise and the general commotion boiled up around us. The air still stank here in the city proper. Once Nylad laughed, har har har har. The sight of three youths beating an old man with sticks struck him funny. The old man reminded me of the Derone, and I wished it was him they were beating. Once Nylad stopped to grab some fruit from a stall. When the owner protested, my bodyguard punched him. Then I protested and made Nylad apologise. Nylad did so with little grace, and stared at me with hatred. The silence between us grew thick and ugly, but after a while he was back to his jovial self again. I think it was the spectacle of two women tearing away at each other with their nails that cheered him up.

Atherton's cover was as a wine merchant. The theory was that a sober man closely associated with alcoholic beverages is more likely to run into people who freely dispense stray information than most others might. He was going by the name of Almjen. As we went along I wondered whether maybe he hadn't been struck down by some awful disease. Everywhere we went the city was the same, stinking and loathsome and squalid, overcrowded and violent and insect ridden. And I wondered whether maybe he hadn't gotten into an argument with someone who'd simply killed him. There appeared to be endless opportunities for death here, and to me the amazing thing was that he'd lasted as long as he had.

We reached the wine district. It was a large square plaza, filled with a jumble of stalls, and a noisy crush of people. I dismounted from Pacesetter and calmed him down as best I could. Then I gave the reins to Nylad, told him to stay where he was, and not to sample from the stalls. He gave me a brief morose nod, and I went off to begin my search. The stink here had a different flavor from the rest of the city. Odors of wine and vomit mixed sharply with the usual smells of piss and sweat and shit. The heat seemed hotter here than elsewhere. And there seemed to be more flies, more flies and more heat, and more stink and more people, all hopelessly entwined and entangled. Poor Atherton, I thought. What a rotten way to make a living.

I shouldered through the mobs and began to ask questions. No one knew who Almjen was. I described him. They still didn't know who he was. He sells wine, I explained. We all sell wine, I was told. Forget this dubious person. Try my wine. I have the best in the city. Sip it, sniff it. I'm trying to find a man named Almjen. There's nobody here by that name. He sells wine. Mine is better by far. He's in his twenties, a man of medium height, of medium build, with a narrow face, and a broad forehead. Never saw him around here. He sells wine. Forget him. My wine is noted for its aphrodisiac properties. No I'm trying to find—

"Discouraging isn't it?" Peter said.

"He was here and he must have left some traces."

"What if he didn't?"

"He must have."

"Is it possible that he wasn't there at all?"

"Unfortunately anything is possible."

"How long are you going to search for him?"

"As long as I have to."

"That could be weeks."

"Months."

"Years."

"Centuries."

I worked my way from stall to stall. No one had seen this person named Almjen. Merchants come and go. Some travel through the mountains to sell their wares, and a number have recently joined the army. I worked my way systematically around the plaza. My soggy but silken toga represented wealth. I was besieged by merchants who wanted to sell me their entire stock. This Almjen isn't here. Just try a sip of my wine. He's in his twenties, of medium height, of medium build, a narrow face, a broad forehead. My wine is the best. I kept on searching. Finally I found someone who'd seen him, the blossoming daughter of one of the merchants. She was a sweet and innocent child with bold eyes, in a thin shift that concealed few of her emerging charms. She spoke right up.

"Almjen the quiet," she said. "He used to have the stall beside ours. A handsome man."

"Do you know where he is?"

"He's not here anymore." She gave me an inviting smile. "You're a handsome man yourself."

"And you sure have a way with the women."

"I must find Almjen," I said.

She pouted. "Ask the Derone then."

"The Derone?"

"His soldiers came for him," she said, "twenty or more matings of the moons ago."

"Uh oh."

"Do you know why they came for him?" I said.

She shook her head. "They came in the night. The next day he was gone. I was very sad. Would you like a drink?"

"I don't think so."

"Our wine is the best in the city."

"Some other time." I left her.

"Now what?"

"I'm going to go back to the palace and nose around."

"The palace is a dangerous place."

"Yeah."

"Is it really smart to go back there?"

"Suggest an alternative."

"You could always give up and go home."

"I haven't got a home."

"You can buy one with the money from this job. CROWN has to pay you for what you've done so far."

"Money isn't the issue."

Atherton is probably dead."

"Probably."

"But you're going to keep looking for him."

"For a while anyway."

"Until they get you dead too."

"Are you suddenly concerned about my welfare?"

"Only aesthetically, not personally."

"Fuck your aesthetics."

"Sure."

He clicked off. A few minutes later *The March of Saul* began to play. Peter was a lot of things, but subtle wasn't one of them. I worked my way back through the crowds to my starting place. Pacesetter was happy to see me. Nylad had found the temptation of the wineshops too great to resist. He was stewed to the gills. Moreover he'd decided he didn't like me at all, and to show his dislike he took a drunken swing at me. I broke his thumb. He stared at me as though I'd doused him with ice water. With his size in comparison to my size, he should have been able to crush me easily. I offered to let him try. Instead he mounted up and, without a word, led me back to the palace.

I whacked Pacesetter goodbye, and Nylad took him away. I got directions to the Room of Joy in the Hall of the Dancing Green Autruth. The same guard was at the door, but the room itself was empty. I stretched out on the bed to do some thinking. Time passed. Peter had put on some nice sitar music. An hour or so went by without any great ideas occurring to me, and then my door was opened by a huge soldier that I didn't recognize. He huffed and he puffed. I sat up.

"What is it?" I said.

"You will come with me now."

"Where?"

"You will come," he said.

"Tell me where."

"The Derone wants you."

"Coming," I said.

We wandered through the corridors, and the armed guards left us alone. As usual I was lost before the second turning. The lamps flickered on the walls, and the carpets muffled our footsteps. We arrived at a door. I could see that it wasn't just any door. The gong out in front of it gave it away.

"Who is this?" the door guard asked.

"The Derone's new seer," said my escort.

"One moment." The door guard hit the gong with his club, and from within the room came an answer. "He's busy."

My escort said to me, "Wait here."

"If you insist," I said.

The door guard hefted his club. "I'll watch him."

"Do that." My escort lumbered off.

The door guard watched me keenly. More time passed. The sitar music had been replaced by something recent and experimental that I thought was tedious and uninspired. I paced back and forth. The door guard watched me as though I was a slow motion ping pong match. I wondered why the Derone wanted me. Time kept passing. Then three syllables rang out from behind the door. The guard struck his own gong once, and told me that I could go in. I got down on my knees. The door was pushed open, and I crawled through it. I felt it bang at my heels as it shut.

"The Derone is mighty," I said. "The Derone is merciful. The Derone is wise. The Derone is—"

"Enough of that ceremony," said the effeminate voice. "You may stand and approach me."

I stood and took a step forward, and then I stopped short. The Derone had company. His room was almost the same as the one I'd just left. It was square, not big, a bed dominating, no windows. The Derone lay on the bed like a desiccated corpse. Around and about were a few chairs, several tortured statues, a crimson carpet, some intricate tapestries, the requisite number of lamps to keep the place lit, and a small gong beside the bed. And a tall man holding a heat gun. I stared at him blankly.

"So you're the seer," the gapjumper said.

I nodded. "Yes."

"Can you actually read the future?"

"On occasion," I said.

"Did you predict that you'd meet up with me?"

"Not exactly."

"I know who you are," the gapjumper said in Basic. "Not your name. But I know who you are. You're from CROWN."

I didn't reply. The language was unfamiliar to me. I continued to stare at him, blankly. The weapon was also unfamiliar. In fact I had no idea that it was even a weapon. This whole affair baffled me. I glanced over at the Derone. The old bastard was propped up on pillows. A blanket was snugged around his waist.

"Well kirlu?" he said.

"I don't understand what this is all about." I was wearing my best bewildered expression.

The Derone gestured at the gapjumper. "He contends that you're a sham prophet and a liar."

"But why would I—"

"He doesn't know who you are," the gapjumper said in Basic. "It was much too complicated to explain to him. He doesn't know who I am either. I told him I was a prophet too."

"What's he saying?" the Derone asked me.

"His language is foreign," I said.

The Derone scowled. "Is it a language of magic?"

"It's the language of dreams," the gapjumper said in the

local dialect. "Those of us who are not sham prophets can speak it. Of course it's foreign to him."

"I am but a simple kirlu," I said by rote. "My dreams come to me in the language of my life."

The Derone said, "One of you is lying."

"Not me," I said.

"Naturally he'd say that," said the gapjumper.

I shrugged. "Because it's true."

"You deserve to die," the gapjumper said. "You've lied to your Derone, lied again and again and again."

"I haven't lied," I said.

The gapjumper was tense. "I'm going to kill you." He waved the heat gun at me.

"Now listen kirlu." The Derone's voice was almost kindly. "You claim that you can read the future, and that your future is to aid me in my conquests. You can't do this if you're dead."

"I'm going to kill you fairly." The gapjumper tossed the heat gun on the bed. "I won't even use a weapon."

"And if you survive," the Derone said, "it will prove that you didn't lie to me."

The gapjumper went into a crouch. "Are you ready?" He was obviously impressed with his own toughness.

"I don't want to fight you," I said to reinforce the impression. "You're bigger than I am. Isn't there some other way we can settle this?"

"No," he said.

I backed away from him, trying to cower convincingly, trying to seem defenseless. He took the bait and lunged at me. I leaned to get out of his path, and succeeded only partially. His fist caught me on the shoulder, numbing the left side of my body. But that put him close and off balance. I smashed the edge of my right hand against the bridge of his nose and felt things splintering. He howled like a nervous multipede.

My left hand was pretty much out of the action, so I hit at his face and neck with my right. He twisted to get beyond my reach. I kept at it. Then he tried to bear hug me, and I slammed the heel of my hand up under his chin, and his head snapped back. His eyes went dull. The whiplash effect had gotten to him.

He let go of me and fell to the floor, moaning and dripping blood on the carpet. His head hung down. He moved in a small blind circle. I'm not sure whether he was seeking me, or seeking a place where I wasn't. He started to get up. I kicked him as hard as I could in the ribs, hurting my toes, and cursing the lack of sturdy boots on this planet. He went down again.

"Get away from him kirlu," the Derone said.

I was panting. "Yes Derone."

"I believe you have told me the truth." The Derone was holding the heat gun, and he swung it towards the gapjumper. "You are the one who is lying."

In Basic the gapjumper said, "I should have killed you sneaky." He choked and spat blood. "This confrontation shit sucks." He raised his head to look at me. "One of these days I'll learn—" he choked again and spat more blood "—I'll learn to control my fucking arrogance."

"Is he praying, do you think?" the Derone asked me.

"Perhaps," I said.

"Prepare to die," the Derone told him.

"So finish me," the gapjumper said in local. "Don't prolong it. Just finish me."

He blazed. His clothes and body hair whuffed into flame almost together. The room temperature rose. I backed away further. The Derone kept the triggerstud down. An odor of searing meat filled the room. The gapjumper was screaming. On the wall behind him, a tapestry caught fire. He tried to crawl away. But his arms and legs were ash, and it was too late for him anyway. The carpet began to burn. The gapjumper stopped screaming.

The Derone let up on the triggerstud, and told me to put out the fires. I singed myself dragging the tapestry down from the wall. Then I folded it over on itself, to smother the flames, and used it as a flail to put out the carpet, which was only smoldering. When that was done, I was filthy, smudged with soot, and breathing hard. I used what was left of the tapestry to cover what was left of the gapjumper. And through the smoky haze, I stared at the old man. Awe was mingled with my great fear.

"Are you a god?" I asked him.

He laughed. "I might be yet."

"You have elemental fire at your command."

"First fire and then the world."

"My Derone." I prostrated myself. "My Derone."

"With your talent and this power," he motioned with the heat gun, "all of the world can be mine."

The floor was pretty messy to be prostrated on. "There is no one and nothing that can withstand you."

"Rise up kirlu," he said, "and I will show you how men may imitate the gods and even surpass them."

I got to my feet gratefully, my eyes still wild with fright, and stood amidst the wreckage. The Derone was lying back on his pillows, mumbling quiet senile nonsense to himself. I brushed futilely at the soot on my silken toga. The air in the room was foul. I felt a bit sick. The smoke hurt my eyes, irritated them, which was fine with me. The tears and redness added to the image I was trying to put across.

"Can you talk?"

"Not now," I subvocalized.

"But you won the fight?"

"The Derone ended it with a heat gun."

"Did you say a heat gun?"

"Yeah."

"The Derone has a heat gun?"

"Call me back later, I'm still with him."

"How many of them does he have?"

"I only saw one."

"Do you think he has any more?"

"Peter I can't talk."

"You're frustrating me, but I understand. You don't want to talk, you don't have to talk."

"I can't talk."

"And you don't have to listen to anything either." He shut down the radio, also cutting the music.

"Oh well," I said aloud.

The Derone quit his mumbling, threw off his blanket, and got out of bed. "Kirlu."

"My Derone."

"Follow me and we'll go to a more pleasant place, where we can examine the future at our leisure."

"Yes Derone," I said.

All of the guards along the way knelt to us. The Derone was an ancient skeletal wisp, even slighter in size than me. I walked a respectful three or four paces behind him, and felt my fingers twitch at the sight of his scrawny neck. We didn't have far to go. After a couple of turnings we came to another door, to another room a lot like the one we'd just vacated. The Derone made himself comfortable on the bed, arranging the pillows and pulling the blanket up to his waist. Then he invited me to sit. I took one of the chairs, and faced him, still projecting terrible fright.

"I wish to tell you about the world," he said. "Have you ever been further than the desert in your travels?"

"No Derone," I said.

"You've never been beyond the mountains?"

"Never Derone."

He gestured expansively. "The world is round, and vast, and full of great wealth. There are so many people, they cannot be counted. In some places a cold white powder falls from the sky like rain and lies on the ground like dust. It is so cold in these places, a man could die from it. Do you believe me?"

"Yes Derone."

He frowned abruptly. "Are you loyal to me kirlu?"

"I worship you," I said.

"As much as you do your lord?"

"More Derone."

He nodded with satisfaction. "I can see that you do. There are traitors everywhere." He shook his head sadly. "Do you comprehend any of what I've told you about the world?"

"Some," I said.

"You will comprehend all in due time."

"Yes Derone."

His tone became anxious. "And now you must tell me something. Do you see my death in the near future?"

"No Derone." I spoke positively.

"In the far future then?"

"I cannot see your death at all," I said.

It was maybe a hazardous thing to say, but it seemed like what he wanted to hear. Megalomania is fed by a desire to be immortal, and he was most certainly a megalomaniac. He lusted for the world, and there was other proof. The Derone traditionally chose his own successor. No one who really expected to die would have chosen such a hedonistic nonentity as I'd seen yesterday to take his own place. The Derone expected to just go on and on forever, and I was perfectly willing to confirm his plans. Of course he was immortal.

"I suspected as much," he said without astonishment. "And you do see me conquering the world?"

"Yes Derone."

He held up his hands, distorted and fleshless. "The man you fought showed me how to take the world in my grasp. But he was a traitor who was using me to gain his own ends. With your loyal aid I will gain those ends myself."

"I live only to serve you."

"The world will be mine," he said exultantly. "And I will share the riches with those who are faithful to me."

"With weapons such as you used before, containing the fire of the gods, no one can possibly stand against you."

He waved that away. "It's the only one like it. I will use it as I did earlier, to execute my enemies, and to display the extent of my power."

"Who was the man I fought?"

The Derone waved that away too. "He's of no consequence. I wish solitude. Call the guard in here."

"Guard," I called.

The guard came in on his knees. "My Derone."

"Treat him as my trusted servant," the Derone said, meaning me. "Do whatever he bids you. That is all. You both may go."

He made a gesture of dismissal. His eyes were nearly closed. In another moment he'd be asleep. But he couldn't admit that he was tired, or show any other signs of human frailty. Such signs would be unbecoming in the immortal master of the world. I got down on my knees with the guard, and we backed out, leaving the glorious son of a bitch to his dreams.

The guard dropped me off in my room after I told him I wanted to be alone to pray and meditate.

"I can talk now," I said. "Peter I can talk."

"Are you sure you feel like it?"

"I'm sure."

"Well I'm not."

"Not what?"

"Sure I feel like talking."

"You don't have to if you don't want to."

He paused. *"Then I guess I will."*

"How's Soraft?"

"Crapped out as usual."

"Ummmmm."

"Ummmmm."

"Did you hear my last conversation?"

"Yeah I heard. The Derone sounds as mad as a hatter. Where did that phrase come from anyway?"

"I have no idea."

"At least he's only got the one heat gun. I shudder to think of what might happen if he had a whole arsenal. Probably the—"

"Wait a second."

"Why?"

"Shhhhh."

There were noises out in the corridor. I lay down on the bed and composed my features. The door to the room swung open, and I sat up to greet the visitor. Besaca was standing there. She was still beautiful and still naked, the female version of the uniform of the day. I smiled at her and she took her hand out from behind her back. She was holding a heat gun.

"Good evening," she said in Basic.

I looked blank. "Huh?"

"There's no need to pretend."

"Come again?" I said.

"You're insulting my intelligence."

"I beg your pardon?"

"CROWN should have known better," she said, "than to pick an agent who's been circumcised. They don't do that here."

I shrugged. "There are some things you just can't help carrying around with you."

"What's going on down there?"

"An aggressive young woman," I said, "whom I presume is the one who gave me away to that other guy, is aiming a heat gun at me."

"Oh."

The girl motioned with her gun. "Ricerick was a conceited idiot. I'm not surprised that you beat him."

"I'd like to go to the toilet," I said.

"Stay where you are."

"And if I don't?"

"I'll burn you down," she said.

"And if I do?"

"The same thing."

"Then fuck it." I gathered myself. "Here I come."

I went straight up in the air, using the bed as a springboard. The girl pressed the triggerstud on the heat gun. My clothes burst into flame. I hit the bed on the bounce, and launched myself at her. She instinctively put up her hands for protection. The gun started to burn through the ceiling, which was a lot better than it burning through me. I slammed into her hard, and we both went down. The gun flew across the room.

I rolled painfully around on the floor, trying to put out my fiery toga. The girl scrambled after the gun and got it. I managed to slap it out of her hand. She tried to snatch it, but I got to it first. She snarled and snatched again. I swiped at her head with it, and she swerved, and the gun barely nicked her. But the threat of it kept her back. We panted and glared at each other, both of us down on all fours. My midsection was a mass of agony, and my nice silken toga was ruined, but at least the fire was out.

"Okay," I said.

She sneered. "Go on and kill me."

"I'm afraid not." I got to my feet very carefully, ignoring the pain as best I could. "Stand up."

She stood with a fair degree of dignity. "Now what?"

"Turn around," I said.

"Can't you kill me to my face?" She got an acre of contempt into every word, and you'd think she wanted to die, the way she kept on insisting upon it.

"Don't antagonize me," I told her wearily. "Just turn around and save the clever comments."

She turned and I took the necessary five steps that separated us and knocked her out. She sagged to the floor with a gasp. Sprawled out like that, she looked innocent, the contempt all gone. But the feelings I'd had for her when we'd been making love were mostly all gone too. Now I had my numbness back, perhaps less than before but back, and that was fine with me.

"*Meas.*"

"I'm busy."

"*But—*"

"Later."

I went to the door, and pushed it open. The sight of my guard lying on the carpet either dead or unconscious didn't exactly shock me. My room was around a turn in the corridor, which was defense enough against the curious. I checked the guard to see whether or not he was still alive. His pulse rate was steady, so he was only unconscious. But I couldn't count on that lasting. I took out my teeth and injected him with a drug, to make sure he'd be out for another couple of hours. That way he wouldn't decide to wake up and stumble in on me at an inopportune moment.

My midsection was really hurting me. I took some anesthetic from my teeth and injected myself. Then I went back into the room, got the girl under the arms, and dragged her over to the bed. She was limp and heavy. I heaved her onto the mattress, and her legs spread wide. A rush of somatic memory hit me, but now the anesthetic was working, somatic numbness for psychic pain. I arranged her more decently on the bed.

All I had left in my teeth were the poison and the truth drug. I extracted the latter ampoule, and reached out to the girl. She coiled suddenly and kicked me with both feet, catching me in the jaw and the stomach. My mind went away to someplace red. I folded up and hugged my erupting belly. My lower teeth had been rammed up into the unprotected roof of my mouth, and I retched and drooled blood and spittle all over myself and the bed. The girl swarmed onto me like a school of starved piranha fish, scratching and clawing and biting and slashing and driving me crazy. I almost had to snap her neck to subdue her.

This time I didn't waste any time in slipping her the needle. Then I stopped to take stock. I was bleeding from a vast number of deep and shallow cuts where she'd gashed me, and the inside of my mouth felt as though it had been ripped open with hooks. All I could taste was blood and phlegm, like a rare steak sauced with liquid copper. But the anesthetic helped to reduce the pain, and I didn't feel nearly as bad as I should have. I felt bad enough though. And I was going to feel a lot worse, as soon as the drug wore off. The prospect of dying in anguish from infection wasn't a very pleasant one. That was a purpose for the poison, to save me from such a fate.

"Peter," I said with some difficulty.

"*I'm here.*"

"I want you to listen when I question this girl, and record it as it comes for future reference."

"Your voice sounds funny."

I spat out a mouthful of blood. "The girl kicked me on the chin while my teeth were out."

I was speaking through splinters of shale. "The girl kicked me on the chin while my teeth were out."

"*Ouch.*"

"How's Soraft?"

"*Sleeping like a baby.*"

"Doesn't he ever get up any more?"

"*Let him alone, he's mending.*"

"I could use a bit of that mending myself."

"*C'est la guerre.*"

"Are you set to record yet?"

"*I've been recording.*"

There was a click and a whoosh, and then I heard me say, "*Are you set to record yet?*" He was right that my voice sounded funny.

"*I've been recording.*"

There was another click. *"See?"*

"You done good." I shook the girl until she opened her eyes. "Can you hear me?"

"I hear you."

"Yes," she said.

"Not you," I told Peter. "The girl."

The girl said, "Girl."

"Sorry Meas."

I shook her again. "Can you hear me?"

"Yes." Her tone was bland and unemotional, her stare was fixed on nothing, she was entirely under my control.

"Tell me your name," I said.

"Name."

I spat out blood. "Tell me your name."

"Name."

"Peter I must be doing something wrong."

The girl said, "Wrong."

"I believe you have to use the question form."

"The question form," I said. "That's it exactly."

"Exactly," said the girl.

"This is all being recorded."

"Yeah."

The girl said, "Yeah."

"Little Miss Echo."

I touched her to reassert control. "What is your name?"

"Catherine De La Mare."

"Now we're getting someplace."

"Try to keep out of this."

"This," said the girl.

I spat more blood. "Which planet do you come from?"

"Grefstyn."

That was interesting. The Grefstyn were still at large, and still causing trouble. I wondered that the planet hadn't been quarantined long ago. But CROWN was a great one for letting her enemies run around loose, the presumed theory being that given enough rope they'd eventually hang themselves. And with suitable provocation CROWN could publicly decry them. A negative press is the most capital punishment of all. I got back to the girl.

"Are you alone on Jsimaj?" I said.

"No."

"Are there others nearby?"

She seemed confused. "I don't know."

"You don't know if there are others nearby?"

"I don't know," she said.

"What precisely don't you know?"

"I don't know."

"Ask her about something else."

"For example?"

The girl said, "Example."

"Their ship."

"Did you arrive by ship?" I said.

"Yes."

"Where is the ship based now?"

"On Tarbah," she said.

I spat more blood. "How many are aboard the ship?"

"Two."

"Are they male or female?"

"Yes."

This time I was the confused one. "Are the people aboard the ship male or female?"

"Yes," she said flatly.

"They probably would be either male or female."

My injuries were no doubt affecting my usual uncanny ability to reason with incisive logic. "I see your point."

"Point," said the girl.

"You may proceed."

The process of elimination was obviously called for. "Are the people aboard the ship male?"

"No."

"Try female."

I spat more blood. "Are the people aboard the ship female?"

"No."

"One of each then."

"Peter please."

"Please," said the girl.

I sighed and swallowed blood. "Is there a male and a female both aboard the ship?"

"Yes."

"Now ask her something important."

"Let me think."

"Think," said the girl.

With such encouragement, I thought, and I said to her, "Are your people aboard the ship monitoring you?"

"Yes."

Her vacant expression changed. The muscles of her face became tense with dismay, and she shut her eyes so tightly that the lids disappeared. Then I realized what was happening. Up in the ship they were jamming her. She put her hands to her ears. But she couldn't hope to quiet the noise in her skull. They were turning the volume up high enough to kill her. It was so loud now that I could hear it myself, a frequency feedback noise, pitched so high it was like the whine of a mosquito.

For her it must have been far above the range of tolerance. The mosquito whine went higher and higher, a remotely wielded scalpel, performing the final fatal surgery on her brain. Why they waited so long, I'll never be sure. Maybe they thought they could learn something useful from my questions. They might even have thought she'd mislead me, and when she didn't they ended the whole thing there. The whine went higher and higher, so high that it almost hurt me. It hurt the girl enough to make her scream, despite the inhibiting drug that was in her. She screamed and writhed and flung herself about, as though in the grip of a massive electrical discharge. And then she died, and that was that.

"Meas what—"

"They killed her."

"How?"

I spat blood angrily, and told him how, and then I said, "There's something I have to do before we can talk freely."

"You have to get rid of our audience."

"That's right."

"I'll be here when you're done."

"Sure."

I looked down at the girl. The wall lamps threw shadows across her relaxed body. Her face was quite calm, returned to innocence. The dead appear to be sleeping, but I fear they dream of darkness. In a way her people had done me a service by killing her. They'd saved me from having to do the rotten job myself, and my fury with them was mainly guilt on a detour. My realization of this only made me angrier. But I still had to do what I still had to do.

A tool was needed. I left the room and searched the unconscious guard. He was carrying a stiletto, a short ceremonial type of blade, in a sheath on his hip. I took the stiletto and went back into the room, and very carefully opened up the girl's throat. Everything kept trying to slip out of focus, and my hands shook as I made the incision. There was almost no blood, just the barest trickle. The dead hardly bleed at all. It's the living who bleed.

The transmitter came out reluctantly, a tiny bright sphere, with an unblemished silver surface. I stared at the sphere for a moment, considering various methods of disposal. Then I decided that simplest was best. I used the haft of the stiletto to smash the delicate mechanism against the stone wall of the room. Maybe that would create some feedback too, and reach her people up in the ship. I sincerely hoped so.

There was one last thing I had to do before I was done. The girl wasn't going to stay in here with me. I squatted down and picked the body up, and tried to ignore my aches and pains and contusions. My flesh was puckering and blistering from the burns. Bent almost double, I staggered to the door, and stumbled through. My burden fell from my arms, hitting the carpet with a muted thud. I leaned against the wall for a few seconds and gulped air. Weariness had overcome my anger. I lurched back into the room, and lay on the bed, and watched the room whirl around me. After a while I was able to speak.

"Peter," I said.

"*You done?*"

"And done in."

"*What comes next?*"

"Nothing."

"*Nothing?*"

I felt really terrible. "Nothing much. This project is over for us. We know the score, and we know the players."

"You haven't found Atherton yet."

"Fuck Atherton."

"You were sent to find him."

"I was sent to determine why he went out of contact, and as far as I'm concerned I did."

"The Grefstyn."

"Uh huh."

"So that's it."

I yawned. "You can radio CROWN with the news. I'll be leaving here as soon as I'm strong enough to meet you."

"Meet me where?"

"In the desert someplace."

"When?"

"Within a day or so if I'm lucky."

"What if you're not lucky?"

"Longer."

"How bad are you hurt?"

"Pretty bad."

"Are you likely to die?"

"I'd prefer to reserve judgment on that."

"Well then aren't you afraid someone else is going to sneak up and try to catch you unawares?"

"Like who?"

"One of them, for instance."

"I don't think there's any of them left down here."

"The girl said she wasn't alone."

"She wasn't alone, she was with me."

"You're making a hell of an assumption there."

I got out of bed with an incredible effort, and collected some stuff from around the room. "My major assumption is that they're running a relatively efficient operation. Efficiency requires a minimum of personnel. They have a man and a woman down here, and they have a man and a woman up in the ship. What conclusion do you draw about the two survivors?"

"Spare parts?"

"My conclusion exactly." I stashed my false teeth, and all the used drug ampoules, and the heat gun, under the mattress, and put the stiletto, after wiping the blade, under my pillow. "Spares for the two down here."

"You're assuming one for one."

"Isn't that logical?"

"But they might not be as efficient as you believe them to be. Your continued existence is evidence of that."

I got back into bed. "Figure it this way. They can't possibly have another man in the palace. A strange man wouldn't last an hour with all the guards and checks and so forth. Plus the Derone only knew about the man he forced me to fight, which also argues against there being another of their men in the palace. Another woman is possible, but not very plausible."

"No?"

I let loose a gargantuan yawn. "Why bother putting another woman in the palace?"

"Why put one there in the first place?"

"To act as a communications link with the ship in case something happened to their front man."

"Something did happen to their front man."

"But probably not something they anticipated."

"You."

"Me."

"Meaning they weren't prepared in advance."

"Not sufficiently."

"And they improvised."

"Inadequately."

"And you beat them."

"Not necessarily." The anesthetic wasn't completely effective, and the pain kept squeaking through. "I set them back."

"What about the two in the ship?"

My limbs weighed a ton. "What about them?"

"They can come after you."

"But they won't."

"You expect them to just sit and wait?"

"I expect them to show some elementary caution." All this debate was tiring. "They don't know how badly I've been hurt, but they do know you'd alert me the minute they landed. They'll worry that I can run and hide and strike at them from secret. The Derone would hide me. He doesn't like them any more than we do."

"So you're safe."

"Either I am or I'm not, and if I'm not, there's nothing to be done, and now I have to go."

"*Meas.*"

"Send CROWN the message."

And then I was gone.

Somebody summoned the palace physician. He was young and intense, and seemed to know his business. I woke up with him working on me. He'd brought a salve for my burns and scratches and cuts, and a foul potion that I drank holding my nose. The salve was cool against my skin though. After he finished applying it, the physician bandaged me up.

"Will I be all right?" I asked him.

"That depends."

"On what?"

"A lot of things." From culture to culture the physician's oath is always the same, to refrain from giving the patient information at all times. "How do you feel?"

"Like a piece of clarowdung."

"The Derone wants to see you," the physician said. "I told him you ought to stay in bed. He told me to take you to him. Do you feel up to the walk?"

"I suppose," I said.

"And he had one other request."

"Yes?"

"He told me to tell you," the physician said, "to bring the fire weapon to him."

"The fire weapon?"

"He told me you'd understand."

"I certainly do." The old bastard wanted to see me because he wanted more power to display, and he must have realized my burns meant a second heat gun was available. "Help me up."

"Here."

The physician gave me a hand. He was tall and thin and stooped, with a perennial grim expression, backed by sharply watchful eyes. I sent him off to replace the toga the girl had ruined on me. While he was gone I reached under the mattress of my bed, and took out the heat gun and the last ampoule from my teeth. My mouth was hurting me less, but my midsection was hurting me more, in spite of the nice cool salve. By now the anesthetic I'd taken was almost totally out of my system.

"*Hey Meas.*"

"Yeah."

"*I transmitted the message.*"

"Any reply?"

"*Not so soon. They probably haven't even received it yet. In the meantime, Soraft is dubious.*"

"About what?"

"*Things in general.*"

"I sighed. "Put him on."

"*Gnarla.*"

"Hello Soraft."

"*How are your wounds?*"

"Not good, how's yours?"

"*Much better.*"

"Glad to hear it."

"*Are you going to be leaving soon?*"

"Just as soon as I can."

"*Will I be able to go home then?*"

"Of course."

"*Can I go home now?*"

I paused for a moment, and then I said, "You're not a prisoner. You can go whenever you like."

"*The boy says I can't.*"

"Why?"

"*He says you'll explain.*"

"Peter did you say that?"

"*I guess I did.*"

The pain in my midsection throbbed, so I sat on the edge of the bed. "I haven't got any explanations. Soraft doesn't have to stay. He can go whenever he likes."

"*No he can't,*" Peter said in a rush.

"Then you explain."

"*He has to wait for you.*"

"That isn't an explanation."

Peter spoke hesitantly. "*The thing is I don't want to make too many landings. I land to drop Soraft off, I become a target, I lose my ability to maneuver. One landing, the one to pick you up, is a risk. More than one landing, one for you and one for him, and the risk is greatly increased. Passing the buck to you was a stall. One landing for both of you is all I want to make.*"

"Why did you stall and not explain?"

"*Because.*"

"I won't take because for an answer."

He burst out. "*I didn't want to seem scared and not wanting to land is chickenshit.*"

"Jesus Christ."

"*You think I'm a child.*"

"Only when you're being childish."

"*Well.*"

"Soraft can you see the risk?"

"*I can see.*"

"Can you wait?"

"*I can wait.*"

"Peter we're all of us scared."

"*Sure.*"

"Shall I run down the platitudes for you?"

"*I wish you wouldn't.*"

"Then put on some music."

"*String quartets?*"

"No no please no string quartets."

He put on some Hans Holterbosch. "*That okay?*"

"Fine." The music was soft.

"*Uh Meas.*"

"Ummmm."

"*Do you think—*" He stopped.

"Go on."

"*Never mind.*"

"Oh go ahead."

"*It's nothing.*"

"Peter."

"*Skip it.*"

There was a soft musical silence that went on until the physician returned with my new toga. "Can you raise your arms?"

"A little bit." I did so. "What's your name?"

"Utole," he said.

Between us we managed to get the toga on me, though my midsection objected vengefully when I moved. The walk down the corridors was an agony, and I had to lean on the physician most of the way. When we got where we were going, I told him to wait outside. Kneeling was far too painful to be borne, so I went into the room on my feet. The Derone was in the bed, blankets heaped to his waist.

"Did you bring the weapon?" he asked.

"Yes Derone."

He nodded. "Now I have two."

"Yes Derone."

"There might even be more."

"Yes Derone."

He frowned. "We have to defend ourselves against them, these people who seek to destroy us."

"Yes Derone."

"Give me the weapon."

"Yes Derone."

He put out his hand, and I passed him the gun, butt first. He smiled happily. I drove my last ampoule into his wrist. He drew back his hand to stare at the stinger, and he started to speak, or to yell for a guard, or possibly just to grab at a final breath of life. But he was dead already, and no sound came out, except for a tiny hiss, and his hand dropped to the blankets.

I shut his eyes for him. Then I uncurled his fingers from around the butt of the heat gun. His hand lay palm up in his lap, like the twisted corpse of an insect. I took and discarded the ampoule, and began to search the room. I searched the bed, and under the bed, and behind all the tapestries, and everyplace else. But the other gun wasn't anywhere in the room. I shoved open the door. The door guard was standing by his gong. The physician was leaning against the corridor wall, intently watching his toes flex in his sandals.

"Utole," I said.

He glanced up. "What is it?"

"Something's wrong."

"My Derone." The door guard streaked anxiously past me and into the room.

The physician hurried in after him, and crossed to the bed, and quickly examined the old man. "The Derone is dead."

"Dead." The door guard was stunned.

I said, "But how?"

"His heart perhaps," the physician said. "Did he die while you were in here with him?"

"We were speaking." I was choked with grief. "He gasped and his eyes rolled back. I shut them and called you immediately."

Utole squeezed my shoulder. "You did the right thing."

"That's good," I said.

The funeral lasted three days. There was much feasting, much lamenting over the deceased, much celebration of his successor. I don't know any of the details, because I didn't catch the show. All the sins of my past life were cited against me, and I spent the three days in a hell of anguish and delirium. In short, my wounds had become infected.

I was wild and frenzied, I babbled, beset by emotional fits. Up in the *Shoten Zenjin,* Peter and Soraft spoke to me, tried to keep me company. I was unreachable most of the time. I broke out into cold sweats, suffered through hot flashes. Utole was with me for hours on end. When he was there I jabbered at him incessantly, and when he wasn't there I jabbered at the wall lamps, at the shadows and the flames, and at the unseen contact ship orbiting above. Sometimes I slept, though never well, and sometimes I screamed. The nightmares were bad, they were very bad, and they were continual.

Somehow I recovered. Maybe it was the disreputable potion that Utole kept pouring into me over my feeble protests. More likely it was despite the potion, but whatever it was I recovered. The monstrous bubble of pressure inside me exploded. Lucidity, or my usual close approximation thereof, returned. When I came to myself I was all alone.

"Peter," I said weakly.

"*You're up.*"

"But not about."

"*How are you feeling?*"

"Lousy."

"*That's no surprise.*"

"Any word from CROWN?"

"*Several.*"

"So tell me."

He paused. "*Can you take this?*"

"I can take anything."

"*You're sure?*"

"Positive."

"*Are you sitting down?*"

"I'm flat on my fucking back."

He paused again. "*I'd better tell you later.*"

"Tell me now."

"*Well okay.*"

"Okay."

"*You ready?*"

"I'm ready I'm ready."

"*Don't excite yourself. Decoded, the return message reads, and I quote, 'Proceed with projected Grefstyn operation. Take planet. Reinforcements not available at this time.'*"

"That's the message?"

"*End of quote.*"

"This is too much."

"*Do you have a reply?*"

"How about, 'get fucked'."

"*You want I should send that?*"

I sighed. "No just acknowledge receipt."

"*Done.*"

"All right."

"*You know something?*"

"What?"

"*They really don't plan on you collecting your fee.*"

"So it would seem."

"*Have you got a next move?*"

I considered for a moment. "I'm going to have to try and convince the successor that he should let me go out and conquer the world for him. But first I need some more sleep."

"*Soft music?*"

"Yeah," I said. "Soft."

But I was gone before the music even began.

Utole was there when I woke up again. He had a knife and was using it to whittle a shapeless chunk of wood. The shavings made a pile on the carpet at his feet. I asked him to fill me in on what had happened while I was away. He told me about the funeral for the old man, and the installation of his successor.

"What do you think of him?" I meant the successor.

Utole shrugged. "The Derone is the Derone. That is who he is. What is there to think?"

"Oh come on," I said irritably. "You must have an opinion of him. You can say how you feel."

"Can I?" Lamplight glittered along his knifeblade.

"Your opinions will stay in this room."

More shavings piled up on the carpet. "Will they?"

"I guarantee you."

"The Derone was your lord," Utole said. "You were loyal to him. He was old, he is dead. Are you loyal to the new?"

I waved my hand. "I haven't decided yet. That's why I want to know what you think of him."

"You are involved in some sort of intrigue here." The knifeblade stopped. "Will you poison him as you did the other?"

"Poison?"

"You talk in your sleep," Utole said.

"Fever speech and nonsense."

"Perhaps."

"But you believed me?" I said.

He resumed his whittling. "I do not believe much to begin with. My father before me was palace physician. He trained me in the ways of treating sickness. The old Derone had him executed after a long lifetime of faithful service."

"Why?"

"For having an opinion," Utole said.

I stared at the dancing spot of light his knifeblade made on the wall. "It's true that I poisoned the old man. I thought he deserved to die. He was evil. You should have poisoned him yourself. You had the opportunity."

"I am a physician, not a murderer." The knifeblade went scrape scrape scrape against the wood. "My father taught me to heal. He didn't teach me to kill."

"Evil is a sickness, and death is a cure," I said. "I killed one so that many could live. When people are dying without any reason, everyone is a murderer, and everyone shares in the guilt. I admit that it's easier to kill through inaction than by the more direct and personal methods, and that it's easier then to push the blame away. But I have good motives for the murders I commit, and when I commit them I do so directly and personally. Can you say the same of your motives and methods?"

"I heal," he said. "That is what I do. I am not a murderer. What do you want from me?"

"Your help."

"To do more murders?"

"No, to save more lives," I said.

Utole would make a fine ally. He sat on the edge of my bed, holding his knife to the lamplight. The light was red and silver along the blade. A gleam of black shone on the hilt. Another dark glow was picked up as a deeper tone across his drawn face, and then shone once again in the triangular profile of his eye. He turned to me.

"I have never been out of the city," he said, "and you must have wandered all over. Are the other places you've seen any different from this one?"

"Some are, some aren't."

"That's no answer."

"Answer me first," I said. "Will you help me?"

"Who are you?"

"You wouldn't want to know."

He pointed the knife at me, as though he wished he could use it. "What are you doing here?"

"Making changes," I said.

"And you want my help?"

"I need your help."

"Impossible," he said.

I closed my eyes. "Thanks anyway."

"You want me to follow you blindly." There was a subtle note of desperation in his voice.

"I want you to leave me alone," I said. "I have things to do, and I have to rest up for them."

He touched my arm. "Drink this."

"More potion?" I could smell it.

"Drink."

I sat up and gulped down the disgusting gunk. "Now will you let me rest?" I lay back and closed my eyes again, and then I heard the scraping of the knifeblade.

"The new Derone is better than the old," Utole said, "in that he seems to have no interest in torture and pain. But he cares nothing for anyone but himself, and for nothing but the gratification of his senses."

I opened my eyes. "Do you know him well?"

"Not very."

"Have you ever had to treat him for anything?"

Utole nodded. "On a few occasions. He gets drunk and falls down a lot, and I've had to treat him for sprains. Once I pulled one of his teeth for him, shortly after he was chosen, about twenty matings of the moons ago. He was the worst dental patient I ever had. He acted as though the loss of a single tooth was the biggest thing that had ever happened to him. Also he's quite a bit overweight. I've suggested a number of times that he go on a diet. But he's healthy, except for his heaviness, and amazingly virile."

"Do you think he has any desire to carry on the old man's program to conquer the world?"

"Matters of state don't concern him," Utole said with a hint of disapproval. "He'll probably surround himself with others of his ilk and let the city go to ruin. Already he's brought a group of parasites and sycophants into the palace with him. The celebration of his office continues unabated. I think it will go on until he dies."

"How did he come to be chosen?"

"The old Derone didn't confide in me," Utole said. "But gossip is that he sought out the most thoroughly depraved person he could find, because he was amused by the idea that such a man would one day have power over all. This successor is fourth in his line. The rest were executed on the old man's whim."

I stared at the moving knifeblade. "Would you be able to arrange a special private audience with him for me?"

"So that you may poison him too?"

"I just want to speak with him," I said. "Could you arrange for the audience?"

Utole shrugged. "I could try."

"Please do."

He got to his feet and handed me the carved block of wood. "This is for you." The carving vaguely resembled an inhuman face.

"Who is it?" I asked.

"Your lord deity," Utole said. "Ytrifg the Inscrutable. Did I fail in creating his likeness?"

The face was treacherous and sly. "No you did fine."

"I thought so." He gave me a long final irresolute look, and then he crossed to the door and went out.

"*Is he gone?*"

"He's gone," I said.

"*Are you going to murder the new guy or not?*"

"I haven't decided yet."

"*Soraft is up. Hey Soraft. Meas has got that young physician running his errands for him now. Here's the plan. Meas is taking the planet over very slowly, by converting your people one by one to his point of view. It shouldn't take him more than a thousand years or so at that rate.*"

"Ho ho ho."

"*Is Gnarla still in the city?*" Soraft asked.

"*Yeah.*"

"*Those people are not my people. My people do not live in the city. My people drive the clarows from the stockades, where they are bred, through the desert to the city marketplace.*"

"*And then what?*" Peter asked.

"*Then we take the money we have earned, and buy*

provisions, and return to the stockades, and purchase more clarows."

"*To drive through the desert to the city again.*"

"*That's right,*" Soraft said.

"*Why not breed the animals yourselves?*"

"*Because this is how it is for us, and this is how it has always been, and this is the way it is done.*"

"*But wouldn't it be better,*" Peter said, "*and more profitable, to be more than just middlemen?*"

"*No.*"

"*It wouldn't?*"

"*We do it the way we do it,*" Soraft said, "*because that is the way it is, and that is how it has always been.*"

"*Circular logic.*"

Soraft spoke loudly. "*Our way is not to be questioned. You don't know anything about us.*"

"*I don't have to know anything,*" Peter said with equal fervor, "*to know that you're wrong.*"

"Knock it off, both of you," I said. "You're giving me a headache. Argue it out on your own time."

"*Our way is not to be questioned,*" Soraft repeated stubbornly, and then there was silence.

"Peter." No response. "You there?"

"*I'm here.*" He sounded resentful. "*That's the thing. I'm here and you're there and I can't see what's going on with you, and more often than not I can't even guess what's supposed to be happening. I'm going out of my mind trying to figure out what you're up to over the radio, and you keep brushing me off and telling me you're busy and I'm bothering you and—*" He paused to inhale.

I refrained from blasphemy with enormous effort. "Peter I realize you're stuck up there. But you have to realize that I'm also stuck down here. I would much rather have our positions reversed."

"*So would I.*"

"But let's be reasonable."

"*You know what I'm going to do?*" he said suddenly. "*I'm going to hit their ship on the moon.*"

"Don't do that."

"I can hit them now, when they're not expecting an attack, and blow them apart."

"Listen."

"I can do it."

He was being asinine, which made me angry. But he was angry too, so I had to be calm. One of us had to be calm. Peter was bored and impatient, and that was understandable. He didn't like being left out of the action, and he could get into things whenever he felt like getting into them, and he couldn't be stopped unless he felt like being stopped. So he had to be convinced.

"Listen to me," I said.

"What?"

"Consider the situation we're in."

"I have."

"But you haven't."

"Oh haven't I?"

My fists were clenched, and I unclenched them. "Will you please just listen to me?"

"Go ahead."

"CROWN wants us to force the Grefstyn hand," I said. "That's why they sent those orders. No one could overtly take the planet before, because that would have involved unconcealed aggression. Presence is legal, interference isn't. The move to take the planet had to be made invisibly, through the natives. It still does. No one wants to get denounced in the Great and General Council for Imperialism. The publicity would be highly negative."

"Uh huh."

"And that sort of publicity," I said, "means a severe loss of prestige in the council chambers. But now that we all know we're here, keeping out of sight is no longer the problem. Now CROWN and the Grefstyn each have the problem of how to make the other look bad. Our job here is to see that the Grefstyn move, and move in such a way as to taint their image. The Grefstyn have to come across as nasty villains, and CROWN as the benevolent protector of Jsimaj. To protect Jsimaj best, CROWN annexes the planet."

"Uh huh."

"Whoever wins the contest is the good guy," I said. "The

Grefstyn wanted to take this place quietly, but things are more out in the open now. Who got here first doesn't matter. Now if they work it right, they can make it seem as though we're the villains and they're the protectors, instead of the other way around. Their best bet is to wait. They wait and hope that we exploit. And when and if the world is nicely subdued and unified, which is what they were after to begin with, then they step in and try to take the package away from us. To best protect Jsimaj, they annex the planet themselves."

"*Uh huh.*"

"They can't bring more ships in," I said, "until they have cause, cause being the proof that we've interfered locally. We can't bring more ships in either, until we can prove the same thing. A newly unified world with aliens on the scene is sufficient proof of an interference. Then whoever wins the final encounter wins the planet. But a premature attack on either your part or their part would only prove presence. The Great General Council would arbitrate. Jsimaj would go to nobody. The council would be the protector. Do you see why we all have to wait?"

"*I guess so.*" His tone was reluctant.

"Do you really?"

"*Yeah really.*"

"You aren't going to hit their ship?"

"*No but I hate the thought of doing nothing.*"

"You won't be doing nothing, you'll be helping me."

"*Helping you how, by playing music?*"

"By being up in the sky where you can see the terrain, and can let me in on what's ahead when we start to march."

"*You can't march at all unless the Derone's successor decides he wants you to conquer the world for him.*"

"He will."

"*Are you sure?*"

"I'll insist."

"*That should do it.*"

I changed the subject. "How's Soraft?"

"*Absorbed in the library.*"

"Try not to bug him too much."

"Do I bug him?"

"Just try to remember that he must be finding this whole affair to be a traumatic experience."

"Okay okay."

"I'm going back to sleep."

"Shall I put on some music?"

"Anything you like."

He put on some John Phillip Sousa marching songs, possibly to inspire me, but I managed to fall asleep in spite of them.

Utole woke me up when he got back.

"What did he say?" I asked.

"He'll see you."

"Privately?"

"Yes," the physician said.

"When?"

"Now."

"All right," I said.

"Are you feeling up to it?"

"I'm fine."

Utole nodded. "Shall I show you the way?"

"Please," I said.

"Come along then."

I got out of bed and struggled into my red and gold toga. "What was his reaction when you told him about me?"

"Very strange," Utole said. "He reacted just as though he'd been waiting to hear from you."

We went down corridors, under lamps, around corners, and past a lot of guards. When we got to the room of rooms, Utole agreed to wait outside for me. I explained to the door guard who I was and what I wanted. He struck his gong with his club, got an answer, and pushed the door open.

My wounds were still stiff and painful, but I crawled in on my hands and knees anyway, trying to make the proper impression. As soon as the door shut behind me, I saw where the missing heat gun had ended up. The Derone's successor had it. He was seated in an ornate chair. Except for us, the room was empty. He waved the gun.

"I'll bet you were curious about what happened to this," he said in Basic, with a slight slur.

"*Oh no.*"

I braced myself. "Grefstyn?"

"Who me?"

"No your cousin."

"I'm CROWN," the successor said. "I'm your goddam contact here. Name's Jules Atherton. What's yours?"

"Belaker Meas," I said numbly.

"*Atherton?*"

"We'd better make sure." My heart had started beating again. "All our knowledge brings us nearer to our ignorance."

"All our ignorance brings us nearer to death," the successor said. "Why are recognition codes always so goddam morbid?"

"Maybe they're supposed to teach us something." I got to my feet and went over and sprawled in a chair across from his.

"*The new Derone is Atherton?*"

"In the flesh," I said.

"*Wow.*"

"Are you talking to someone?" Atherton asked me.

I pointed at the ceiling. "My pilot."

"Ah."

"*Fucking Atherton.*"

"Yeah," I said.

"*Incredible.*"

Atherton laid the gun down on a table next to him heaped with a vast and colorful assortment of fruits and nuts and meats and wines. "Sorry if I frightened you with that."

"*With what?*"

"A heat gun."

"You should have seen your face," Atherton said with a chuckle. "I thought you were having a goddam coronary."

"Ummmmm," I said.

"*Were you really that frightened?*"

"Not quite."

"*But almost?*"

"Not even almost."

"*Were you trembling?*"

"Peter."

"*What?*"

"Shut up."

"Your pilot?" Atherton asked me.

"That's right."

"His name's Peter?"

"Yeah," I said.

"Hi Peter."

"*Hi.*"

"He says hi," I told Atherton.

"Is he a little punk with a great big complex like every other goddam pilot I ever met?"

"No he's okay."

"*Gee Meas I didn't think you cared.*"

"Shut up," I subvocalized.

"*I like you too.*"

Atherton gestured broadly at the laden table. "Could I offer you a bite to eat?"

"I'm not hungry." I stared at his bulky form. "You know with all that extra weight and that beard, you don't look very much like your pictures any more."

"The price of the good life." He poured out wine from a flask to a goblet and swigged it. "Would you like a drink?"

I shook my head. "No thanks. I was sent here to find you. You went out of contact. How come?"

"My cover here was as a wine merchant." He took a long swig from the goblet. "After I arrived I naturally set out to make the best goddam product I could. Wine's been a hobby of mine for years. I chose my cover because of that." He took another swig. "The wine I made and sold was the best around. Excuse my lack of modesty. My fame spread. The other goddam merchants were jealous. Eventually my wine was noticed by whosis. And he sent for me."

"With soldiers."

Atherton took another swig. "That was just his way. So I came and we learned we had things in common—"

"Things in common," I said incredulously. "What kind of things could you have in common with him?"

"Various tastes and appreciations." Atherton refilled the goblet from the flask. "I didn't really approve of him of course."

"Swell."

"But we got friendly, and here I am."

"Why no contact?" I said.

Atherton took another swig. "My goddam equipment got smashed accidentally. It was one of those things. You sure you won't join me in a drink?"

"I'll pass this round."

"Beefs up the blood," he said.

"No thanks."

He took another swig and spoke with immense enthusiasm. "I'm going to have them locate me a decent goddam tobacco substitute and grow a few acres for my own personal use. Hypnotherapy doesn't matter. I can beat it. Just imagine, Jsimaj cigars." He took another swig. "When you've been away from civilization as long as I have you'll feel the same way. I've been here for a year and a half. This goddam extended observation duty is a drag." He refilled his goblet. "Come on and try some of this. My own recipe. Best there is. Put hair on your chest and a sparkle in your walk."

I shook my head firmly. "I'd rather not."

"By the way," he said. "I was sorry to hear about your getting burned by that goddam girl."

"Sure."

"Still hurt?"

"I'm better every day," I said. "Do you remember a Captain Gangot of the Derone's army?"

He took another swig. "Don't think so."

"The one who brought me in for interrogation."

"What about him?"

"I just received orders from CROWN," I said, "that I have to go out and conquer the world. I'd like to see Gangot in charge of the force I'm going to bring with me. Will there be any trouble taking care of that?"

"Nope."

"How many men are there in your army?"

"My army." He took another swig, draining the goblet. "Has a nice sound to it. Atherton's army. Atherton's army. Atherton's army." He refilled the goblet. "Nice alliteration."

"Lovely."

He took another swig. "You ought to try this stuff. A couple of goddam sips won't hurt you."

"I'd just as soon not," I said. "Those burns I got still make me queasy, and I haven't been eating much, and wine on an empty stomach would nauseate me."

"You're probably right."

"So how many men are there in your army?"

"There's thousands of them." He took another swig. "Thousands and thousands. The Derone had a big goddam recruiting program on, and he told me about his plan for world conquest, but he didn't specify his troop strength, and he didn't allow me to ask any questions. He mentioned his new advisor once or twice, but I wasn't introduced to the man. Later I saw the goddam heat gun."

Atherton took another swig. "That was after the man was dead and you'd taken his place as advisor. The Grefstyn had manufactured the heat gun, the goddam curved flanges on the grip were the giveaway, and I figured that then you were with CROWN." Atherton gestured. "Your appearance here, and your actions, were too explicit, too opportune, and too familiar. You had to be with CROWN. The Derone had me under guard though, and I wasn't able to confer with you. Keeping me under guard was his usual practice. He wanted me to remember that I was his goddam slave more than I was anything else.

"The Derone was a pig." Atherton took another swig of wine, and stared in my general direction. "I was his goddam pampered libertine house pet, and some of the things he made me do were incredible. He used me like I was a goddam living dildo. I told you we were friendly, but that was entirely on his side. He was also unpredictable from moment to moment and I was lucky he never had me executed. You did me a great favor rubbing him out." Atherton winked at me. "I know you did it. You were the only goddam one with him when he died, and I know you were trained to kill. I can see that quality in you, because I was trained to observe. Not much gets by me." Atherton took another swig. "I swear that I would have snuffed him myself if I'd had your training.

"He was clever though, and he might have caught me. My reward would have been an exceedingly slow death." Atherton shivered. "The thought of that was unbearable to me. I was trained to observe and blend into the background. You were trained to kill and to anticipate torture, and you're prepared to suicide rather than die in agony. I've met a lot of goddam agents from your department. You have a poison tooth that can save you when the going gets too rough to take. I had one of those too, my lower left bicuspid."

Atherton drained and refilled the goblet. "All of the guys in my group used to joke about visiting the goddam dentist, and how we'd better not eat any rock candy or hardened women afterwards. One drop of soup went into the tooth and got sealed back up." Atherton motioned with the goblet. "Then we'd joke about chewing on people we didn't like, and when we hit bone the tooth would break and the poison would get them. But we couldn't actually conceive of using the goddam soup on ourselves. The idea was preposterous. Soup was standard issue, like our special ID belt buckles, nothing really serious. And every six months we'd return to the dentist routinely to see that the goddam seal was still properly sealed."

Atherton took another swig of wine, and aimed his gaze at the carpet. "Prior to this one my longest assignment was for seventy-five days, and after I'd been here for over a year I began to worry. I started to poke my tongue at the little goddam cavity in my bicuspid where the seal was. My tongue could feel the outer edge, the sharp outer edge of the cavity rim, and the smoothness of the seal inside." Atherton took another swig. "The cavity was shaped roughly like a goddam relief map of Africa. I got so I was poking at it constantly, making sure the seal was still in place. The tip of my tongue was rubbed raw by the goddam sharp edge, I was poking at it so much, and my tongue puffed up and became insensitive. Then I couldn't feel either the cavity or the seal any more. I went into a panic.

"The poking had grown to be a goddam compulsion with

me, my assurance that I was still safe from the poison." Atherton took another swig, "I'd turned into a monomaniac, and I was well aware of the fact. But my compulsion had to be satisfied. I kept trying to poke at the goddam cavity with my swollen tongue, and all that accomplished was to make matters worse." Atherton squirmed in his chair. "I was going insane. My fingers weren't delicate enough to feel the outline of the African map, and besides I was afraid that I might inadvertently break through the seal with one of my fingernails, although I'd trimmed them so short that most of them bled at the goddam quick. And still I kept poking at the cavity with my tongue. The habit pattern of doing that was ingrained too deeply for me to stop."

Atherton took another swig of wine. "I was even able to make myself believe I could almost sort of feel something kind of like the map of Africa, but way down inside me I knew I was lying because of my terror and desperately clutching at straws. And my goddam tongue got progressively worse. There was barely enough room in my mouth for it, and the lie I was telling myself became more and more obvious. The terror consumed me. I had to drink a fantastic goddam quantity of wine just to get to sleep at night." Atherton glanced at the goblet, and took another swig.

"I had native assistants run my business for me. My mouth was so full of tongue, and my mind was so full of confusion, that I couldn't talk coherently to anyone. I went into seclusion. My goddam reports to CROWN were sporadic." Atherton drained and refilled the goblet. "This went on for quite a while. Finally I had to accept that things were as they were. The lie was a lie, there was no salvation. The seal that held back the goddam poison in my tooth could break open at any time, and there was absolutely nothing I could do to delay or prevent that from happening." Atherton shrugged. "There was nothing I could do. My mind cleared very soon after I came to a genuine goddam intellectual acceptance of this."

Atherton took another swig. "An emotional acceptance was much more difficult, but I flatly refused to give in to despair. I spent about a week going over the problem. Extracting the goddam tooth was out. There was too good a possibility the strain might break it." Atherton gestured negatively. "Extraction was definitely out. My swollen tongue was still compulsively poking at the cavity, and I began to eat a lot with the right side of my mouth to distract myself. The deadly tooth was on the left side, and I didn't want to take any chances. CROWN could have saved me, but my request was refused. I was told there was no one available who could relieve me. That was when I went into a drunken rage, and smashed my goddam communications equipment beyond repair." Atherton took another swig. "I regretted the move, but it was irrevocable. Then I came up with the thought that all the goddam poking I'd done and was doing with my tongue might somehow in some way have weakened the seal. I hadn't even considered that before, but the idea ended my compulsion at last. The potential danger made me stop. A few days later my goddam tongue was back to normal.

"I still had to drink myself into a stupor every night to sleep, but I was beginning to function again while I was awake." Atherton took another swig of wine. "I drank a lot during the day too, and I ate more than I ever had, and I gambled away a goddam fortune, and I went through hordes of women. The thing was to cram all my life that remained with as much as I could. And my range was a fairly wide one, because my goddam wine business was making me rich." Atherton grinned. "I could afford to indulge in virtually any sort of recreation that interested me. The condemned man was eating as many last meals as the goddam warden would let him.

"Then one morning a small band of soldiers came for me, and without any comment as to why, they fetched me away from my goddam house and brought me here." Atherton took another swig. "The Derone thought my wine was magnificent, and he wanted to tell me how much he liked it. He'd also heard about my reputation as a swinger, and wondered what kind of a goddam person I was. We discussed this and that, and ate and drank, and had a few more meetings." Atherton made a wry expression. "The next thing I knew I'd been appointed his goddam successor. The one before me was dead, and a replacement was needed. The Derone didn't give me a choice. He wanted me, and I was his."

Atherton took another swig. "Given a choice I would have

turned him down. My exalted position was notorious for being insecure, with the four goddam successors before me having all been executed. But once I was there I decided I had nothing more to lose, and so I might just as well take the devil by the horns. I went to the palace physician, who's about the most sincere goddam individual in creation, and told him I had a colossal toothache, and he was going to have to operate. He remarked disparagingly on my girth, which he does whenever he sees me, and went off and got his goddam tongs. I was all hyped up for the operation, very tense and drunk and apprehensive." Atherton chuckled. "The physician must have thought I was a first class goddam sissy. Here I was acting as though my life was at stake, when as far as he knew this was only a simple extraction."

Atherton took another swig. "I instructed him over and over on how I wanted the tooth pulled, until he was ready to let me do the goddam job myself. The extraction positively had to be done in a single take, out of my mouth and gone with no repeats or slipups. I was very goddam emphatic about that. And I told him not to exert any pressure with his tongs unless he was certain he had a solid purchase on the tooth. Then he was to yank the goddam thing out and away from me as fast as he was able." Atherton took another swig of wine. "So he reached in and got hold of the tooth and out it came. All my goddam poking must have loosened it or something. It just came out effortlessly, and I didn't feel a thing." Atherton laughed. "Of course I was too goddam drunk to feel much anyway, but that was the neatest tooth extraction I've ever had.

"And I still have the tooth." Atherton took another swig. "Would you like to see it?"

"Sure," I said.

The tooth was in a brass locket, on a chain around his neck underneath his toga, and it looked exactly like a tooth. "How about that?" He grinned proudly as he displayed it.

"Beautiful." I didn't bother to tell him that all of my own poison had been used up to make him the toast of the town.

He tucked the tooth away, and took another swig. "Sometimes things do work out for the best."

"That's what keeps us going."

"Yes indeed."

I said, "Will you see that Captain Gangot is placed in charge of your army?"

"Captain Gangot?"

"The soldier who brought me in for interrogation."

"I remember him," Atherton said. "A fine goddam officer. You want him in charge of my army."

"Is that all right?"

Atherton took another swig. "Anything you say."

"And see that he knows I'm his boss." I stood to go. "Gnarla the kirlu is the name I'm using here."

"Gnarla the kirlu."

"Okay?"

Atherton frowned. "Are you leaving me now?"

"I'm tired," I said. "I need rest. We begin our campaign to take the world tomorrow. Don't forget. Captain Gangot in charge of the army. Gnarla the kirlu in charge of him."

"I won't forget."

"Good."

Atherton took another swig. "Can't you stay for a while?"

"I'm half asleep."

"Could we get together tomorrow?" There was more than a hint of wistfulness in his voice.

"Tomorrow I'll be busy," I said. "Captain Gangot and I will have things to discuss. We have to get the army ready. Plans will have to be laid. There's going to be a lot to do."

"I understand." Atherton took another swig of wine, and tried to conceal his disappointment. "You have your goddam orders. I'd like to hear the news from home of course. But that can wait. Tell the goddam guard outside to come in when you leave. He can send for Captain Gangot at once."

I crossed to the door. "See you later."

"Take it easy."

"You too."

And then I left.

I sent the goddam guard in the corridor in to see Atherton, and Utole led me back through the maze to my room. My bed was very comfortable. Utole undid my bandages, and examined the burns. I told him about the approaching campaign. He smeared his cool salve on my midsection, and wrapped some clean new bandages around me.

"You're going to start tomorrow?" he said.

"In the morning."

"But you aren't ready."

"I'm more than ready," I said.

"You're in no condition."

I stared at him steadily. "I'd like you to come along. You asked me once what the world was like. Come and see for yourself. Maybe you can even keep me alive in the process."

"The world," he said.

"Will you come?"

He nodded. "I'll come."

"Wake me up in the morning," I said. "Not too early. Sometime just before noon would be fine."

"Couldn't you put this off for a week?"

"No I couldn't."

"Here drink this." He produced more potion.

I groaned and drank. "What is that stuff anyway?"

"Medicine."

"Why does it taste so horrible?"

"Because if it was delicious," he said, "no one would believe it was curing them. Medicine has to taste horrible. Being sick isn't supposed to be fun."

"Get out," I said.

He got out.

"*Meas.*"

"I'm trying to sleep."

"*That Atherton sure goes on and on once he gets going. But I guess he was glad to have someone to talk to.*"

"I guess."

"*Hey.*"

"Yeah?"

"*I haven't got a poison tooth.*"

"No kidding?"

"*I wasn't issued one.*"

"So complain."

"*I will when we get back.*"

"Peter."

"*What?*"

"I'm trying to sleep."

"*Don't you think you'd be better off waiting a week like your buddy there says you should?*"

"I want to be done with this."

"*Just wait a couple of days then.*"

"We start tomorrow."

"*Oh well.*"

"Good night."

"*But the sun is shining.*"

"Good night."

He sighed. "*Good night.*"

Flashback II

They got me for illegal information retrieval. Somewhere along the line an informer must have informed on me. There was no other way that I could have been caught. When my company heard about it, they promptly threw me to the wolves, and denied all knowledge of my activities. Better that I should be blamed than them was their attitude.

The trial was a patent absurdity. The defense and the prosecution had come to an agreement before the whole thing even began. I was told that they had me, that I should plead guilty, and trust to the mercy of the court. The results of the trial were strictly a foregone collusion.

There was no jury.

The judge took the bench.

I pleaded guilty.

The judge banged his gavel.

He sentenced me to five years of solitary confinement at hard labor on the planetary prison of Bloomer in the Burbank System. He said that I had the right to appeal, and that a pardon could be obtained by approval of a Petition to Colonize, as provided for under the Reilly and Hawthorne Statutes.

He banged his gavel again.

143

Five years.

Claire and I discussed it briefly before they took me away. We both felt that we should apply for colonization. But she was pregnant then, and that made things difficult. You can't colonize, because you can't travel through neostasis, during pregnancy. She promised she'd make an application as soon as the baby was born. Then she cried and kissed me.

I went off to Bloomer and dealt with guano.

Six months later I was paroled to Hermes in the Bradford System with my family.

There were two hundred and ninety colonists, about a third of them children. Our own baby was a girl. Claire had named her Carol Ann, which was fine with me. I'd always thought babies were ugly, but Carol Ann was a special case. She took only the best from Claire and me. She was medium dark, with soft brown curls, and bright green eyes. Her face was exquisite. I could hardly wait for her to get old enough to call me daddy.

We spent that first year building the colony from the ground up. The next thing to do then was to put ourselves on a paying basis. The main money crop on Hermes was gems. I went to work as a miner, up in the hills every day. Claire taught school. In the evenings we'd hold each other and make our plans. We'd play with Carol Ann, we'd visit the neighbors, the neighbors would visit us. Life was slow and regular and full.

Three years after we got there, Claire and I had an argument. We didn't have many of them. This day Carol Ann had done something wrong. I don't remember what. I'd slapped her diapered fanny and sent her away. She'd run to her mother in tears, with the tale of my brutality. Claire had come back at me with a comment. The timing was very bad. My work had been going poorly. I lost my temper. Claire lost her temper too.

The words weren't important. They were just variations on a theme. I shouted and Claire shouted, and I shouted louder, and Claire shouted louder still. In the end a solid wall of fury had been erected between us, through which no sensible exchange could possibly pass. Anger has a logic of its own.

I didn't want to go out on that note, but adrenalin had

taken me over. I slammed the door instead of slamming Claire. I got into my hoverjeep and drove too fast to the cave in the hills. I was sure there were gems in that cave. Another few centimeters of digging and I'd have them. I was sure of that.

I sat for a moment and fumed. The sun would be down in an hour or so. Fog was rolling in off the lake. The settlement below me looked as remote and unreal as a woodcut. The houses we'd built, the roads we'd paved, the power plant, the church and school, they all looked unreal.

I took the jackhammer and scoop from the back of the jeep, and strode to the rear of the cave and got busy. After a while I began to feel more like myself. The anger seeped away. Claire would have supper ready when I got home and Carol Ann would be quieted down. The argument would be over and done with. Claire wouldn't continue it, and neither would I. You learn how to live with someone. When you care you learn how to live with someone right. Claire and I both cared.

I heard thunder.

The sky was clear.

I could see the sky from where I was, a blue centerpiece at the front of the cave.

But there was thunder.

I took a puzzled step towards the entrance of the cave to see what was going on.

And then I saw the flash.

And the roof fell in.

When I regained conciousness I was half buried and in total darkness. My eyes hurt and my first thought was that I'd been blinded. I didn't want to be blind. My second thought was Claire Carole Ann Claire Carol Ann and a fearful sense of loss. Because I knew what that flash had to be. There was no mistaking a nuclear detonation.

I tried to get my bearings. The scoop was still in my hand. I used it to get the rubble off the buried part of my body, and started to dig my way out of the cave. I was lucky. None of my bones were broken. My eyes hurt me terribly. I couldn't tell whether or not they'd been burned out. The pain could have been caused by dirt.

I didn't want to be blind. But I wasn't sure that I wanted to see either, if the sight that I thought would greet me outside was there. I managed to dig my way out of the cave before the air went bad. And I wasn't blind. And the sight that I was most afraid of was there.

It was impossible to tell where the exact center of the blast had been. But the houses we'd built, the roads we'd paved, the school and the church, were completely destroyed. They'd been flattened and scattered and razed. I could see that much without any trouble, through the mushroom mist of smoke and debris.

I read a book once about the effects of a nuclear explosion. The thing that had struck me wasn't the legion of dead, nor the utter devastation, nor even the frightfully mutilated survivors. I'd sort of expected all that. What had struck me was a single isolated fact. The book had said that the white hot brilliance of the fireball had somehow caused shadows to be permanently etched on the hard surfaces of streets and walks and the sides of buildings. My wife and daughter and neighbors and handiwork, you might as well say my entire world, had turned into echoing shadows, permanently etched on the hard surface of my memory.

Shadows from a flash.

And echoes of thunder.

I wished I hadn't left them angrily, and more than that, I wished I'd been with them when they died.

I sat down in front of the cave entrance, and aimlessly beat the ground with my scoop. The sun was just setting. I ran through my mind the things I would have said to Claire when I got home, the simple everyday things that wouldn't have been in any way extraordinary. We would have eaten our supper. I would have put Carol Ann to bed. She would have asked me to tell her a story. I tried to think of which story I could have told her. She knew them all better than I did.

Eventually I was picked up and decontaminated. An affable engineering type explained to me what had happened. The reactor in our power plant had gone off. But everyone was sure that the failure had been due to something quite trivial. This sort of thing was really very rare. The affable engineering type seemed to feel that the rarity and triviality were the most important aspects of the event. It took four people to drag me off him.

Eighteen of us had lived through the mishap. We were brought back to Earth and sent to a displaced persons compound for interim processing. The compound was actually a jail. I was there for ten weeks. The others were processed and gone and I was still in there. I brooded, I broke down images that were already broken, and when they were small enough I sifted through them, and searched for some grain of meaning. In the end they were dust. I drew my numbness around me like a cloak. Finally the Bureau of Extraterrestrial Administrations gave me a call. They offered me a way out of the jail, and something new to think about. They offered me a job.

I took it.

Part Three: The Campaign

Pacesetter was there to greet me at the palace steps. I'd wanted to see him the first chance I got, and as usual our reunion was a wet and happy one. Utole and I walked him down to the river. The air was fresh with a tang of salt from the ocean. A mild breeze was blowing in over the seawall, and gulls were sailing the cloudless sky. The sun was as hot as ever.

I was dressed in my durable kirlu robes again, and under the robes was a bulky layer of bandages. My bells and holy cord had gotten lost somewhere, but when fortune wills it one must do without. The robes were my traveling garb. Utole had changed from silk to a toga of coarse material that reached to below his knees. Both of us were sweating a lot. Under my bandages I sweated even more. And I itched there, and I couldn't scratch. But I was glad to be up and around and outside. The palace had been making me feel claustrophobic.

Our army was drawn up smartly in ranks and files, in the middle of the open farming land by the river. I leaned against Pacesetter and surveyed them. There seemed to be about a thousand men in the task force. Their clarows were herded together in a large group, on the bank of the river near the cavern in the mountain. Utole stared out across the field and made no comments.

After a while, Captain Gangot, now Commander Gangot, joined us. He rode up with two of his aides. His promotion hadn't made him any more jovial. When I told him that Utole would be coming along on the journey, he asked the physician if he was prepared to ride to the ends of the world. Utole confessed that he'd never actually learned to ride at all, but he added that he was game to give it a try. Gangot raised an eyebrow at me. I shrugged. Gangot ordered one of his aides to loan Utole his multipede to practice on. Utole took the reins and gave the beast a dubious frown.

Then Gangot explained that we had a problem. The problem concerned our army's nearly one thousand clarows, and the river that ran through the cavern, which was the only access through the mountain, which was the only access to the world we were out to conquer. There were some complex logistics involved in the transportation of all those armor plated mutated pale green giant lizards upstream on barges against the river's natural current.

"Can it be done?" I asked.

"It can be done," Gangot said.

"How long will it take?"

"Perhaps a day."

I glanced at Utole. "That means that we won't be able to start our march until tomorrow."

"At the earliest," Gangot said.

"Then you'd better get things moving."

He nodded. "Will you review the troups?"

"Not me," I said. "I'm no officer in this army. You're their new leader. You review them. I'll be over there."

Over there was in the shade of a spreading tree. I still wasn't at my best, or even my second best, and the sun was still ultra hot. The thought of going out into the field to review the troops was my idea of a fine job for somebody else. Gangot wheeled his multipede about, and rode off to do his duty. I went and sat down with my back to the tree. Pacesetter stretched his neck, and munched on some leaves. I told him not to eat all my shade, and he snorted and kept on munching.

"This delay is to your benefit," Utole said to me. "You get an extra day of rest."

I grinned at him. "And you get an extra day to practice riding your clarow."

"Yes that's true." He didn't sound enthusiastic.

"You might as well get at it."

He stuck a foot into a stirrup and swung aboard, and sat in the saddle tensely, hanging on tight to the high front and the reins. "Now what?" His expression was strained.

"You really should try to relax," I said. "Then there'll be less likelihood of your falling off, and less likelihood of your getting hurt if you do."

He loosened up a fraction. "Like this?"

"More."

"Are you sure?"

"I'm sure," I said.

He loosened up another fraction. "Enough?"

"Are you comfortable yet?"

"I will never be comfortable on one of these."

"Try riding him around a bit, just to get the feel of him." I indicated the reins. "You steer with those. Pull to the left to go left, to the right to go right. It's not very complicated, about on a par with lancing a boil. Reach out and tap the clarow here—" I indicated the auditory area "—to get him going. Haul back on the reins to make him stop. Got all that?"

Utole grimaced. "I think so."

"You control the speed," I said, "by the number and pressure of the taps. Tap lightly once, and you go slow. Tap twice and harder, and you go faster. Tap three times and fairly hard, and you go like the wind. I advise one light tap for beginners."

"One light tap," he said.

"Just until you get used to the animal."

Utole hesitated for a moment, then gave the signal to go slow. His multipede took off at a sedate stroll. The young physician tensed up again the instant he got into motion. He sat there trying to figure out whether he should continue hanging onto the saddle with both hands and let the animal steer, or whether he should screw up his courage and take up the reins and steer the beast for himself. After a brief period of indecision, during which the multipede calmly plodded on in a bearing towards the orderly herd by the river, Utole managed to find a compromise. He removed one hand from the saddle, and cautiously pulled the reins to the left.

The multipede turned obediently and began to go around in a neat little circle. Utole waited until the animal was more or less pointed in my direction. Then he simply dropped the reins, and took hold of the saddle again. The multipede straightened out and headed back. I did my best not to laugh. But before they got to me, in a rash burst of confidence, Utole grabbed at the reins again, this time with both hands, and was soon turning his mount first one way, and then the other. His face bore a look of intense concentration. The multipede seemed indifferent to the whole affair.

"Peter," I said. "Soraft."

"We're here," Peter said.

"Well you're missing a truly classic sight."

"Utole's riding lesson?"

"Yeah."

"Is he getting it on?"

"Tentatively."

Soraft said, *"How do you feel?"*

"Not too bad."

"Your burns?"

"They're still kind of stiff."

"Avoid exertion," Peter said.

"I'm sitting under a marvelous tree of some sort, and I'm soaking up oodles of shade and fresh air."

"That's the way."

"Meanwhile Pacesetter is nonchalantly devouring all the leaves he can get at without actually climbing the tree for them."

"Doesn't he know that defoliation is banned by at least a dozen separate interplanetary treaties?"

"I didn't have the heart to tell him."

"Shame shame."

"Where are you?"

"Directly above your fucking army of conquest. We could bomb them out of existence from here if we wanted to."

"Now remember those treaties you mentioned."

"But nobody else does."

I grinned. "Speaking of which have you heard anything from those guys on the moon?"

"Not a murmur."

"Then put on some lazy music and let me laze."

He put on something that curled around my brain and purred. I went back to watching Utole cope with his clarow. His newly won confidence was gaining momentum. He reached out and tapped the multipede twice, and the animal picked up speed. They were doing about twenty kph. Then Utole pulled the reins to the left, but he pulled just a trifle too hard. I should have warned him about that tight turning ratio. The multipede swerved sharply, legs going in a blur. Utole flew out of the saddle to land on his shoulder with an audible thud.

I waited to see what would happen. Utole wasn't hurt at all, but he was embarrassed. He checked my reaction to his fall. I waved at him casually. He got up and dusted himself off, and got back in the saddle again. I was pleased to see him lean forward, and give the multipede two taps, instead of a nice safe one tap. And away he went.

On the river things were in motion too. The clarows didn't like it very much, but they were being packed five to a barge, and the barges were being poled through the mountain cavern. I could tell that the animals didn't like it by the ungodly amount of noise they were making. The shade of my tree was an excellent vantage point from which to view the entire operation.

The sun moved in the sky, as suns do, and the day wore on. Utole shifted his multipede into third gear, and he raced the animal around like a maniac. He tore back and forth in the area in front of me, so I'd know that he had his act down pat, and he seemed to be having a hell of a time for himself. Pacesetter gave up on my tree, and began to graze in the field. I spent an idle moment wondering what Atherton was up to back at the palace. But there wasn't enough doubt as to what he was doing to make speculation worthwhile. Now and then I dozed.

Some people from Klask'an arrived to audit the business on the river. When nobody chased them, they stayed around. More people joined them. The planted field had been shredded by the army's passage across it, and now it began to look like a brokendown picnic ground. The word of a festival must have gotten out, because half the city showed up. Some of the menfolk even went so far as to shout instructions to the sweltering soldiers. After this had become a bit tedious and prodigal, the shouters were pressed into temporary service, and they sweltered while the soldiers took a break. The clarows continued to make more noise than anyone.

More people arrived and not many of them paid more than token attention to the transport problem on the river. They brought their children along and their pets and so forth, and mostly they gossiped and sang and visited and traded things. And Utole put on a riding exhibition for anybody who cared to watch, though the field was a mite too congested for some of the fancy feats he was attempting. But there were no serious accidents. Chalk that up to the people's habitual skill at dodging clarows, rather than to any spectacular adroitness on Utole's part. The sun moved past its zenith and down, pervading the long afternoon with a holiday glow.

I dozed some more, and dusk descended. The thousand army multipedes, with only a few exceptions, had been barged upriver. And most of the city people had gone home. Fires marked the locations of those who were staying on. Pacesetter grazed in the field not far from me, a dark shape against the greater dark shape of the mountain. Utole rode by me once or twice, and then he reined in. He had some things with him. His expression was moderately cheerful for the first time since we'd met. He swung down from his multipede, and sat on the ground beside me.

"There's really nothing at all to riding a clarow once you know how," he said.

I didn't tell him that a saddle was a lot better to learn on than an insubstantial blanket. "There's really nothing much to anything once you know how," I observed instead, with my customary sagacity. "But I have to admit that you looked pretty good out there."

He nearly smiled. "And you got another day of rest in spite of yourself." He handed me a skin full of liquid. "Here's something for you to drink."

"What is it?" I said. "More potion?"

"Drink."

"But I've had enough potion to last me forever."

"Just try this," he said.

I tasted it warily. It wasn't potion, it was wine. The skin was full of wine with a sumptuous and biting flavor. I thought that if this was Atherton's celebrated product, I could see how he'd gotten rich and famous from it. I sipped the wine and passed it back. Then Utole asked me whether or not I'd eaten that day. I was suddenly very hungry. He produced a bag of meat and vegetables, and another bag of wood for a fire. I could have hugged him.

We cooked the food and ate in something like a companionable silence. My false upper teeth hardly hurt my tender palate at all. The stars were out. One of the moons rose, I don't know which one. The Grefstyn ship might have been up there waiting, but I couldn't see them and they couldn't see me. We were invisible to each other. Yet there were energies that drew us together as surely and inexorably as hydrogen and oxygen are drawn together to become water. And the political energies that united us now and made us conspirators were as natural as water, and equally naturally, would be as volitile as hydrogen and oxygen apart, when our purposes no longer coincided. But that was just some more idle speculation. Commander Gangot rode up before Utole and I were through eating.

"We've established a camp on the other side of the mountain," he said to me.

"By the forest?"

"It could not be otherwise." He didn't swing down from the saddle. "The forest grows everywhere."

"So I've heard," I said. "Tell your men they can take their ease tonight. Tomorrow we'll be moving out."

"My men will be ready."

I nodded. "From here I'll be going back to the palace. Where will you be?"

"With my men," Gangot said.

"When I show up tomorrow we go." I had a thought. "Have any of your soldiers ever been beyond the mountain?"

He was way ahead of me. "Several were merchants before enlisting in the army. I plan to use two of them as guides."

"That's very good commander," I said. "Would you care to join us in our meal?"

He didn't budge. "I eat with my men."

"I see."

"Will there be anything else?" he said.

"No that's all."

"Tomorrow then." He turned his multipede and rode off across the moonlit field, looking so damn military that I wanted to give him a swift kick in the uniform.

"Humph," I said.

Utole passed me the half empty wineskin. "He doesn't seem to like you much."

"He doesn't like the idea of me being his boss." I took a drink and passed the wineskin back. "I'm a civilian, I'm a kirlu. I'm not his kind."

"Are you anybody's kind?"

"My own," I said. "And you?"

"Ask me after tomorrow," Utole said. "That's why I'm going with you, to find out the answer to that question."

"Oh?"

"Yes."

We finished eating, and I said, "I appreciate this, the food and wine, the consideration."

"Someone had to feed you." Utole collected the various leftovers and stowed them in bags, then scattered the embers of the fire and crushed out the sparks. "Race you back to the palace?" He boarded his multipede, and sat there poised.

"I don't think so." I got to my feet, "And is that any sort of a challange to make to a patient who's been lingering on death's doorstep?"

But he was gone before my last words were out, riding across the field at top speed by the light of the moon. I called Pacesetter to me. He came with a quiet snort. I leaned against him for a moment, and stared at the starry sky. There was so much of it. The second moon was rising. Pacesetter nudged me with his snout. He understood. I took his reins and led him back to the city. Tomorrow was soon enough for anything.

To—

—morrow.

We went down to the river in the morning, down to the cavern that was full of echoes, and the dark silver sheen of wet rock. From the bank I could see all the way through to the other end of the tunnel. Shadows moved on the river current. I thought about another cave on another planet far away from this one, where the sky had been a bright blue centerpiece at the front. But that thought was one of the things I tried not to spend my time thinking about any more.

"I hope you got a decent night's sleep," I said to Utole. "Before this expedition is over you might forget what sleep was like."

"My clarow refuses to get onto this barge," he said.

"Watch me with mine."

Pacesetter was an old hand at getting onto things. I threw his reins over his head, and escorted him onto the barge, which a soldier with a pole held stable. Pacesetter followed me on with perfect docility. For him that meant compliance with wailing. I told Utole that there was more to clarowmanship than being able to stay in the saddle, that one must inspire the animal's trust and devotion and love and respect as well.

I put my arm into Pacesetter's mouth to illustrate the point. The multipede quieted down at once. Utole looked at us. Then he looked at his own multipede, with the twelve legs planted firmly on the bank. Utole pursed his lips. I smiled encouragingly. Utole scowled and put his arm in his multipede's mouth, and with enormous care edged him onto the barge. The animal followed submissively.

"There," Utole said with a sigh.

I patted his back. "Now wasn't that easy?"

"No."

"It wasn't?" I said.

"Those fangs."

"Harmless."

"But are they?" he said.

I patted his back again. "Usually." "All right," I told the soldier with the pole. "Let's go."

Inside the cavern the echoes were louder, and every sound was a fierce exclamation. Our polester grunted as he pushed us along against the current. Utole and I kept our respective arms in our respective multipedes' mouths, and the animals remained placid on the unsteady flatbottom barge. The flowing river carried glints of sparkle past us, and after the temperature outside, the damp coolness of the tunnel came as a shock. When we emerged on the other side of the mountain, the temperature change was a shock again.

And then there was the forest, which was actually a jungle, at least in my estimation. I'd been prepared to expect this, having absorbed the reports on the place. But still the sight of it jolted me. The interior underbrush was so dense that the sunlight could barely penetrate, and millions of years of hard radiation had taken a dreadful toll. The trees were savagely maimed and twisted, and interwoven with endless gnarled vines. The vines trailed evil gray moss that hung like ancient voluminous curtains.

But the worst things about the jungle were the ubiquitous orchidlike flowers that grew high and low, apparently thriving anywhere that their roots could take hold and suck nourishment. They seemed to be somehow predatory. Their colors were wild and deranged, a violent assault on the eyes. They were dizzily vivid wherever the light touched them, more and more loathsome and ominous further back. Their predominant colors were yellows and purples and reds, the colors of bruises and weals and open sores. But even more ominous was the lack of noise in the jungle. And deep within the clandestine interior dimness there was movement.

Utole and I coaxed our multipedes off the barge and onto the riverbank, where they rejoiced at having the certainty of dry land underfoot once more. A thousand other clarows were gathered on the bank. Their riders were with them, ready to ride on command. The whole army was camped on the sloping ground between the river and the mountain. Across the river was the forest, patiently waiting there for us. I turned away from it.

The soldier who'd poled us through the cavern tied up his barge next to several others. His multipede was tethered to a bush, of which there wasn't much left, just a leafless skeleton of twigs. The soldier swung into the saddle, and beckoned to Utole and me. We rode along with him to the head of the army, where Gangot was squatting with a couple of his men. They all stood up to greet us, and Utole and I dismounted. Our polester rode off. Gangot stolidly introduced his two men as Parell and Mexag.

Parell was the taller of the pair. He was a thin man with a sardonic manner, and he bowed slightly at the mention of his name. Mexag was rolypoly and deferential. He sported a weedy little fringe of a beard that gave his round features a clumsy sort of cuteness. Neither of them had a crossbow. They were obviously the former merchants who would act as our guides.

"I'm Gnarla, a kirlu," I said. "This is Utole, a physician. Is there a path we can use to get us through the forest?"

"Unfortunately not," Mexag said.

Parell said, "We'll have to make our own."

"What did you use before?"

"A path," Parell said, "which has since closed up. Any path that is made here will close up again after a day or so. That is the way of this forest. The wounds heal as with a living thing. I've been through here on four occasions, and each trip I took was with a small group. The small groups are best. A force the size of ours is bound to attract unwelcome notice."

"That's true," Mexag said diffidently.

"But our force is probably large enough," Parell said, "to deal with the unwelcome notice we attract."

Mexag nodded. "Also true."

"The profits are great on the other side," Parell said, "but so are the dangers in getting there. Many have died in this forest. It is full of deadly creatures whose single desire is to kill and feed. They like the flesh of men. And there are other dangers as well that you might never recognize until too late, such as innocent looking expanses of sand that can swallow an entire army like ours alive."

"Can't we go around the forest?" Utole asked.

"Too big," Gangot told him. "We'd lose a week, perhaps more. We have to go through it."

"To save time," Utole said, "we lose men. I don't understand that. Less men would make us weaker, and an army has to be strong. Are we really in all that much of a rush?"

Gangot glanced at me. "Are we kirlu?"

"Yes," I said.

"But why?" Utole asked me.

I passed the buck to someone not present. "Because the Derone is eager to have this thing done quickly." The motive I gave him was mine of course. "The will of the Derone brooks no discussion." I turned to Parell. "When you were through here before, did you take a special route, or did you just enter the forest anywhere?"

"I always enter at the same place." Parell smiled ironically. "But whether it's safer to enter there or not I couldn't say. The man that I first went through with went in at that place. Now I do too. I imagine that he himself was also taught the route by whoever he went through the forest with first."

"Are we far from this place?" I said.

Parell shook his head. "Not very."

"Commander Gangot," I said. "When can we start?"

"At once," he said.

I mounted Pacesetter. "Then let's get going."

"All right kirlu." Gangot bawled out a series of orders and the camp came to life.

"Do you think," I said to Parell, "that we can get through the forest before nightfall?"

He considered the position of the sun. "We might be able to. The size of our force will slow us down, but we still might get through by dark. Then again we might not. I wouldn't want to bet too much either way."

"Neither would I," Mexag said.

I watched them as they mounted their multipedes. "What if we don't get through by dark?"

"We'd better," Parell said. "The forest is dangerous by day, but it's lethal after the sun goes down. We'd better get through before then."

"I was afraid of that," I said.

Utole and I rode behind Gangot, still between river and mountain. Parell and Mexag came next, and then came the army. The troops must have reached back a kilometer or more, even with all of them riding five abreast. There wasn't much in the way of conversation. Utole rode at my side, sullenly trying not to sulk. He seemed to feel that this project was somehow inhumane. As usual I felt lousy and hot and uncomfortable. My bandages were chafing away at my mid-section, and I still itched and still couldn't scratch. So I wasn't inclined to coerce Utole into talking to me. And Gangot seldom spoke to anyone without a definite reason.

Parell and Mexag however debated various merchandising and sales techniques, and the feasibility of burning out a wide section of the forest, and of keeping the area open for use as a trader's highway. That last would have to be done sooner or later anyway as a matter of routine, to make possible the regular traffic necessary between the city and the conquered districts. I'd brought a heat gun along with me for emergencies, but it wasn't designed for such extensive use. And I didn't want to just whip it out and set fire to things in front of everybody unless I absolutely had to.

The world we were out to conquer was mainly on this continent. On Earth Alexander had taken more world than we had to take here. But that was Alexander, who invented the concept. In addition to this one, Jsimaj had three other continents. None of them was worth the trouble of conquering, because none of them had any kind of a civilized culture, and none of them sat on deposits of high radioactivity.

And none of them had ever had any contact with this continent. Jsimaj's two moons caused powerful tides that tended to severely limit ocean travel. So this was the continent on which to operate. Our scenario for world conquest and universal brotherhood was really the simplest one available. Take over the most developed part of the planet, centralizing the government as much as possible, and then put that government into a box. No other method had ever worked out any better.

"Peter," I subvocalized.

"Meas is that you?"

"Now who the hell else would it be?"

"Speak up."

"I'm subvocalizing."

"Oh."

"Are you reading me?"

"Fuzzily."

I coughed and spat phlegm. "How's this?"

"Try burping."

"Do you or don't you read me?"

"I read you, I read you."

"Then count up what we have to take over."

"I've already counted. You have about sixty villages and hamlets or macbeths or whatever. The inhabitants are mostly peasants and like that, not exactly what you'd call a warrior population. They ought to be easy."

"There have been peasants in the past who have held off armies bigger than this one with nothing but dogged determination and a few farming implements, and who proved themselves to be more than adequate when it came to defending their real estate against all comers."

"No shit."

"Gnarla," Soraft said.

"Hello there."

"How long will this take?"

"The campaign?"

"Yes."

"Not too long I hope."

"I want to get back to my people. I've been studying your books on animal husbandry. They confuse and upset me."

"Too much new information," Peter said. "New information that doesn't match up with the old."

"I just want to go home," Soraft said. *"I live in the desert. These quarters are too confining. I can't get used to them."*

I felt a real sympathy for him. "I've been confined too, and I know what you mean."

"*The campaign,*" Peter said. "*How long?*"

"That's anyone's guess," I said. "But I can give you a rough idea of what we're up against. Our earliest strikes shouldn't be too difficult. We'll have the element of surprise on our side. But after that the going will undoubtedly get heavier. And there's another problem."

"*What?*" Soraft said.

"Supervision," I told him. "We take the land. Let's say we take it with a minimum of fuss. Okay, then we have to hold it. We can't merely take a place and move on. We'll have to leave some soldiers behind at each village. We have a thousand men to begin with. By the time we get to the village number sixty, our forces will be in a sadly depleted state."

"*There's also a likelihood of there being some battle casualties,*" Peter said helpfully.

"Yeah."

"*From what you're saying,*" Soraft said, "*I get the impression you haven't got enough soldiers to go around.*"

"Not nearly enough. But there is a solution. We can supplement our men by recruiting more men from among the conquered villagers themselves. They ought to be willing to go out and conquer someone else, because that would put them on the side that wins the wars. Everybody won't feel that way about it of course. Resentment is sure to keep a lot of them from joining us, but we can offer rewards and adventure and romance to those who do. We should find sufficient recruits."

"*What if you don't?*" Soraft asked.

"Then we're fucked," I said. "But we'll know that fairly soon. And if we lose a big battle we're fucked. In which case we all pack up and go home. Stay tuned. The end is in sight. Can you wait just a little while longer?"

"*I suppose so,*" Soraft said.

"Peter."

"*I'm here.*"

"Would you pipe down some music?"

"*You want to hear anything special?*"

"Holterbosch."

"*Soft and unobtrusive.*"

"Exactly."

The music came on. We continued to ride along the riverbank. Utole was silent, Gangot was silent, the forest was silent. Even Parell and Mexag were silent. The soldiers behind us conversed in low tones, and their multipedes snuffled and snorted a bit. The river was shallow here, and gurgled over rocks. But that was all background noise. The silence seemed louder. The air was full of tension and a hushed expectancy.

Pacesetter swayed from side to side. A gentle wind began to blow. The trees in the forest creaked, and I could smell the flowers. The scent was rotten and overripe. We rode on. The sun was higher and hotter, but the wind was cool on my face. I was slouched in the saddle. The reins were slack between my fingers. Finally Parell called out to tell Gangot that we had come to the place he knew.

Gangot held up his hand to halt the soldiers behind us. The forest here looked the same to me, but the river made an eccentric turn to mark the spot. Gangot ordered a group of his men to dismount, and go into the forest ahead of us, and reopen the path with their swords. They crossed the river, which swirled around their knees, and started to hack. The rest of us took a short break.

Utole and Gangot and Parell and Mexag and I, and several of the officers, splashed in the river for about twenty minutes. While we were doing that the army spread back and back and back, narrowing down to a double file for the push through the forest. At the end of the twenty minutes, we all mounted up again, and rode across the river. The splashing had really refreshed me.

But the forest was dim and steamy and swamplike, and filled with sounds and slitherings. We were assailed by insects. Branches and leaves brushed at us as we passed. Cobwebs threw clammy nets over our faces, and clung like a bad reputation. The scent of the flowers was very oppressive here. Pacesetter shied away from things in the dirt that I couldn't see. And the deeper we went, the more lush was the forest. Above us the hanging moss grew thick and close. The sun was a memory, the sky was a dream.

Our pathmakers swung their swords.

Hack.

Chop.

Cut.

Slash.

We progressed slowly.

There came a scream from somewhere not far behind me. I glanced back and saw a soldier fall from his saddle.

"Keep going," Parell said urgently. "Don't even stop to pick him up. He's lost."

I sat transfixed. "What got him?"

"That doesn't matter," Parell said. "Just keep going and pray there are no more ahead of us."

Utole was stunned. "That soldier."

"The things in this forest kill," Mexag told him. "The soldier is probably done for."

"I'll see," Utole said.

He tried to turn his multipede around, but the path wasn't wide enough. Pacesetter and I hemmed him in on one side, and the forest hemmed him in on the other. We heard more screams, wild and hoarse, screams of agony and terror. Utole sprang from the back of his multipede, and Gangot grabbed at his arm to restrain him. Utole jerked away.

"Stay here," Gangot said.

"But I—"

"Snakes," someone shouted.

Someone else shouted, "Tree snakes."

"Snakes."

"Watch out."

"They're dropping down on us."

I stared up and saw leaves and ropy vines and hanging moss and shadows, the perfect cover for a death that struck without warning again and again. There was nowhere to run, there was nowhere to go. I pulled my cowl up over my head and hunched my shoulders. My muscles clenched and unclenched spasmodically along my spine. Finally the shouts ended. I raised my head, and Utole hadn't moved.

"We got them all," someone said.

I looked around. "Tree snakes." I felt unstrung.

"We must have gone under a nest," Parell said. "Our presence here disturbed them."

"Their venom is fatal," Mexag said.

Parell nodded. "No one ever survives it."

"Come on," I said to Utole. "You can't do anything. There's nothing you can do."

He hesitated a moment, then mounted up. Our path-makers swung their swords, and we advanced, riderless multipedes and all. I could hear a frightened and rebellious murmuring from the soldiers behind us. Gangot dismounted and moved back down the line on foot, ordering and inciting and stimulating the men to keep on.

I was glad that Peter wasn't asking me questions, or making his usual wise comments up in the ship. My nerves were frazzled. Maybe he was able to figure out what was happening to us down here, and maybe he felt that I had enough troubles without his adding to them. And maybe he was asleep at the switch. But whatever the reason, I was glad he was quiet. The music continued to play.

Hack, chop, cut, slash. We kept on. I wished that I'd brought some insect repellent with me. The forest seemed to have an unlimited supply of pests. They dove on me, bit me, got into my eyes, my nose, my ears and hair. They crawled up my legs under my robes. They were after me everywhere. I was losing my mind trying to cope with them. Suddenly—

I don't know what it was. It looked like a lion of some sort, but I've never seen a lion that huge. Somehow I hadn't thought the forest could have any really big animals. There was too much close solid growth. But this thing slipped through the trees and brush like a vagrant breeze with fangs. It was monstrous and swift, beautiful with a kind of dread beauty, and almost as large as a multipede. Its head was enormous, its body proportionate, orange and tan, and it had no mane.

It came from my left without a sound. I was lucky I saw it in time to get the hell out of the way, or I would have been killed when it swiped at me with a giant taloned claw. I didn't stop to think about it. I just flung myself off Pacesetter's back, and more or less into Utole's arms. As I did so I heard the claw rake across my multipede's armored hide.

Pacesetter reared in dismay. The cat tore a huge bloody patch from the multipede's soft white belly. Pacesetter howled and struck out with his own claws. But the cat evaded him gracefully, and the bloodied talons hit again, ripping the multipede open still more. Pacesetter wailed with grief. His distress was communicated to the other multipedes nearby, and their riders tried desperately to calm them all down.

I stood rigid at Utole's side and watched the fight, frustrated by my inability to affect the outcome. I took my heat gun from under my robes, but I didn't press the trigger stud. Pacesetter would have been burned in the fire too. Finally the multipede managed to grapple with the monstrous cat, and they both rolled over into the underbrush locked together. The cat was snarling, kicking with its hind legs, tearing with its fangs. Pacesetter couldn't quite get at it.

But his own legs were many, and he knew how to use them. His own claws were sharp, and so were his fangs. The match was nearly an even one, grace and speed versus weight and power. But the cat also had the carnivore's ferocious instincts, as opposed to the herbivore's usual meekness. The fight went on and on. They rolled and thrashed in their deadly embrace. Neither animal gave way. Then Pacesetter got a good purchase, and snapped the cat's sinewy neck. The cat went limp. Pacesetter just lay down and panted.

The heat gun was in my hand. Pacesetter was dead from his wounds, even if he was still moving around. His misery was as obvious as the thing I had to do for him. But I noticed that Parell and Mexag were staring at the heat gun. I'd taken it out automatically when the fight began, it being the only kind of weapon that I had with me. Now I put it away and borrowed Utole's knife.

I went over to Pacesetter and knelt beside him, and I really believe that he recognized me. His tongue came out to lick my face. His mild green eyes were open and vulnerable, and all I had to do was go in through one of them. My hand was shaking, but I had no choice. Pacesetter blinked at me. I put my arm into his mouth, and told him how brave and fierce, how intrepid and stalwart he was. His eyes were full of trust, and my hand was still shaking, and I still had no choice. I did my duty with the knife. Then I stood up, and turned my back.

Parell and Mexag came over to where I stood.

"What was that weapon you had?" Parell asked me.

"Weapon?"

"The odd one you keep in your robes."

"That isn't a weapon."

His expression was dubious. "No?"

"No," I said.

"I thought it was."

Mexag said, "So did I."

"Why?" I said.

Parell made a vague circular gesture. "Perhaps because of the way you were holding it."

"It's not a weapon," I said. "It's a talisman."

"Ah," Mexag said.

"A protective charm."

Parell nodded. "Of course."

"My sister gave it to me," I said.

Mexag tugged at his beard. "May we see it?"

"Not right now," I told him. "I don't feel well. I'd like to be alone for a while."

"Certainly," Parell said.

They went away.

The news of Pacesetter's death was passed back down

the line, and Gangot brought one of the riderless multipedes up to the front for me. I rode the animal, but he wasn't the same. Pacesetter had been funny and foolish and I missed him. I subvocalized to Peter about the way he'd died, and Peter was very surprised at his heroism. Soraft explained that multipedes could be just as heroic as anyone when their survival was at stake. Peter agreed that survival made for a dandy incentive. They got into a discussion of the topic, and I asked to be included out. The music came back on.

Parell and Mexag spoke together in tones too low for me to hear, and now and then I'd catch one or the other of them looking at me. I didn't like that. Gangot told Utole about the seven or eight cats his men had gotten on the trail behind us. After their multipedes had been calmed, the soldiers performed quite admirably. The cats had been wiped out. Besides Pacesetter, we'd lost one multipede, and that was all. We sustained a few scratches and so forth, but nothing that Gangot considered too serious. And the men were in much better spirits now than they had been since the encounter with the snakes. We kept on riding.

Our pathmakers changed off once or twice. I tried to stay alert, to watch all around me. I didn't want to get caught unawares. The insect pests continued to assail me in relentless droves. I felt hot and sweaty and tired, and my midsection ached and itched. Then the forest began to thin out, and the day got brighter. I could see the sun reflecting off suspended dust particles in the air, and within a couple of minutes we seemed to be riding through a golden mist.

Maybe the radioactivity wasn't as active in this area, because things were less warped than before. The plantlife here was more natural in appearance, and I could hear birds trilling in the trees, not that I have any great love for birds. There were even less insects to be warded off. Our pathmakers quit all their hacking and chopping and cutting and slashing, and they mounted up and rode their clarows along with us.

We were out of the thick of it, but the men behind us weren't, and wouldn't be for some time yet. We would have to make camp beyond the forest, and wait until our forces were all together again. But there was genuine cause for celebration, at least for those of us at the front.

I was ready to breathe the well known sigh of relief when they ambushed us. There were a lot of them. They were either apes evolving into men, or men devolving somehow back into apes. They were covered with matted dull brown hair. They were squat and brutish and broad at the beam, and they carried clubs as big as the nearby tree trunks.

Being a noncombatant I scrambled off the back of my multipede, and went to ground amidst a spray of pretty pink blossoms. I called out to Utole to join me there. He took one look at all the apemen boiling out of the forest and did so. Mexag joined us there too. But Parell swung his sword at the creatures with an unexpected zest, while Gangot and the other soldiers mainly used their crossbows.

The apemen were doomed from the outset. A few of them died at swordpoint, but most didn't get that close to us. The majority of them were simply potshotted with crossbow quarrels before they even got into the fray. They were mechanically slaughtered by technology. Clubs weren't enough against crossbows, and the apemen never had a chance.

Utole and Mexag and I had to dodge overexcited multipedes, while the merciless battle raged about our ears. And there were ants on the ground, mean and shiny, black and omnivorous. I hate ants. I hate little things that crawl all over you in large voracious numbers and feast on your flesh. So as the bodies hurtled by overhead, Utole and Mexag and I squirmed among the blossoms, covered with tiny bodies of our own. I'd abolish ants if I could.

Meanwhile the battle raged on. The multipedes wailed, the apemen roared, the soldiers yelled. All was confusion and tumult. One of the apemen fell to the ground next to me. He was alive, but not very. I took his club away from him, and hit him until he lay still. Give the ants a new victim, divert their attention.

But ants notwithstanding, the apemen were slaughtered.

I don't know how many of them we got. They just came and kept on coming. They fought with supreme and total valor against what they must have thought of as a threat to the sanctity of their domain. In the end they all were killed except for the mortally wounded, and those weren't going anywhere. The soldiers finished off the last of them without any trouble. Technology triumphs again.

Our losses were fairly small. Half a dozen or so were dead, and about twice that were injured. The dead we buried quickly. And the apemen we left to the care of the forest. We got ourselves together, collected our used crossbow quarrels, and continued on our way. In a while we came to open land.

The sun was waning, but we were here. The plains were spread out before us with tall sweet grass, and straight and glorious trees that sprang from honest untainted soil. I sagged in my saddle. The sight would have moved me more if I hadn't felt quite so exhausted. My first day out, my first day of travel anyway, had been grueling. And I still had ants.

"Peter," I subvocalized.

"*Yeah.*"

"Can you see us now?"

"*Is that you coming out from under the trees?*"

"That's us."

"*You sound tired.*"

"Only because I am."

"*Well maybe you recall me and Utole and Soraft and everyone else in the world suggesting that you take it easy and rest up a bit before you went dashing off in all directions like Star Admiral Brisk or somebody.*"

I reined in my multipede. "Like who?"

"*Star Admiral Brisk. He's a substitute father image us youthful rovers of space are supposed to emulate.*"

"Oh."

"*He's a stern but kindly galactic daredevil with a crusty exterior and a heart of gold. A type. He has this pilot*

*sidekick named Dinky Lamont Schickel, who has to bear
the brunt of his endless paternal advice."*

"Dinky Lamont Schickel?"

*"Cute and cuddly and not too bright. Another type.
Brisk has to keep clueing him in on what to do about
things. When we start our training they encourage us to
vicariously participate in this fantasy for retards."*

"Why?"

*"Service orientation. It's pretty sickening stuff, but the
adventure part's okay."*

I was picking the ants off myself and discarding them
one by one. "How far are we from the nearest village?"

*"Twenty kilometers or so. I guess nobody wanted to
build too close to the forest."*

"You can't blame them for that."

"Nope."

"Any obstacles between here and there?"

*"Some multipedes grazing in the grass. But I'm sure they'll
get out of your way. Other than that nothing. Except of
course the wall."*

"Wall?"

"The wall around the village."

"So they have a wall." I crushed an ant vindictively
against my saddle. "What kind of a wall?"

"High and fortified."

"That's just fucking terrific."

*"They probably put it up to defend themselves from the
wandering nasties of the forest."*

"Probably."

A short distance away Parell and Mexag were talking
together confidentially. Mexag was staring at me. I nodded to
him, and he smiled blandly. More and more soldiers were
emerging from the forest, and they had already begun to set
up camp for the night. Gangot was organizing the operation.
Utole had found himself some injured to tend, and was
merrily dispensing potion and bandages to them. From their
expressions I got the distinct idea they would have preferred
more apemen to his potion anytime.

"You there down there?"

"I was thinking."

"About what?"

I glanced over at Parell and Mexag. "We have a couple of former merchants for guides. They've been taking an uncommon interest in me. I was wondering what, if anything, I should do about them."

"You could always ease your mind by murdering both of them in their sleep."

"That's a bit extreme." I considered. "I don't know. I might just be feeling paranoid."

"A little paranoia's good for you. Keeps you on your toes. You live a lot longer."

"But too much paranoia ruins your judgment."

"How much is too much?"

"Too much is when you act too soon and too extravagantly after you've leaped to a doubtful conclusion."

"Meaning you aren't going to ease your mind by murdering those two guys in their sleep."

"No I think I'll wait a while and see." I scanned the horizon. "Is there a lake or stream or river near here?"

"Face the sun."

"I'm faced."

"Turn obliquely left."

"I'm turned."

"Go that way about a kilometer and you'll find yourself asshole deep in a pondful of lily pads."

"Thanks."

I signed off and went and got Parell and Mexag, and the three of us went and got Gangot. Then we all sat down and discussed our strategy and tactics for the morning. That was when Parell and Mexag learned of my occasional ability to read the future, because there was no other way I could explain my knowledge of a terrain I'd never seen before. They reacted to this information by exchanging two of the blankest looks imaginable.

I also mentioned the pond. Gangot sent one of his men to check on it, and by the time we'd finished our discussion, the man was back with word that the pond was there. He figured it was big enough to accommodate fifty bathers. Gangot went off to divide his men up into groups of that size, and I grabbed Utole and told him that if we were fast we'd beat them there.

We were and we did. I stripped off my filthy sweaty robes, and Utole unwrapped my filthy sweaty bandages, taking only a few cubic centimeters of skin along with them, and I dove into the pond with a shriek. Utole dove in after me. And for half an hour we soaked away the grit and the grime and the ants. Then we washed all the clothing and bandages thoroughly, and set them out to dry while we snoozed on the bank.

Groups of soldiers came and went, and eventually darkness came too. The bandages were wrapped around me again, and my robes were put on, and supper was ready back at the camp. We ate and Utole went to tend whoever else needed any tending. I turned in. The ground was hard and cool and moist with dew, and even more restful than a palace featherbed. And the next thing I knew it was morning.

The walls around the village were made of wood. At my suggestion Gangot ordered a squad of his men to attach dried grass to their crossbow quarrels. Then we rode out across a planted wheat field that was otherwise empty in the meagre light of dawn. When we got to within an effective range, the soldiers set fire to the grass, and shot their quarrels into the walls, and the walls burned down quite nicely. Clouds of harsh black smoke rose like industrial waste into the clear blue morning sky.

Unfortunately the village was also constructed of wood, and the wind blew the fire and fanned the flames, and the village inconsiderately burned down too. That gave us about four hundred angry and consternated refugees, stomping around in the cinders that used to be their homes. I knew exactly how they felt. But at least they weren't in any mood to fight us, maybe because we'd destroyed their reason for fighting.

"*Well done Meas*," Peter said sarcastically. "*You've just gone and conquered your first village. Too bad there isn't anything left of it for you to take over.*"

"I'll hire Jiminy Cricket," I said, "when I need someone to act as the voice of my conscience. Now what the hell am I going to do with all these homeless people?"

"You could kill them."

"Don't be ridiculous."

"Oh I'm ridiculous am I?"

"Peter."

"I didn't decide to burn down their village. You can take credit for that one yourself."

"The fucking wind shifted."

"You always have an excuse. But get this. I spot the targets, you knock them over. That's the arrangement. I've done my part. The rest is up to you."

"Yeah sure."

I stared out across the field. I was standing alone not too far from the fire, leaning against my new multipede, which I persisted in thinking of as a stranger. The smoke was already dispersing on the wind that had caused so much damage, and the clouds of black were turning to wispier traces of neutral gray. This exercise really hadn't taken very long. Once the village got going it had burned down fast, no doubt a lot faster than the villagers had taken to put it up.

"Gnarla," Soraft said.

I sighed. "Do you intend to berate me too?"

"No I have a thought for you."

"Okay but be civil."

"You might move the homeless people along with you to the next village and quarter them there until they can rebuild."

"How far away is it?"

"About five kilometers," Peter said. *"I think that's a damn good idea, even better than killing them off."*

"I've seen the next village from here," Soraft said, *"and it's big enough to hold them."*

"Are you praying kirlu?" someone said behind me.

"Huh." I whirled to confront Parell and Mexag astride a pair of multipedes. "Hey."

Parell smiled. "Giving thanks, I imagine, for our victory. One should never forget to give thanks."

"Who's with you?" Peter asked.

"Look Parell and Mexag," I said by way of informing him. "Don't do that again."

"Do what?" Parell said innocently.

"Sneak up on me."

Parell was taken aback. "Did we startle you?"

"We apologize if we did." Mexag was most contrite.

Parell nodded. "Commander Gangot sent us to get you. He appears to be having some trouble."

"What kind of trouble?"

"He can tell you better than we can," Mexag said.

Parell gestured. "He's over there."

"All right." I mounted up and we rode towards the wreckage, and I let the two former merchants get ahead of me, which seemed like an improvement on the last place they'd been.

"So they're sneaks."

"Ummmm," I said thoughtfully.

"That's not very sporting of them."

"Not very."

"They ought to be taught a lesson."

"Definitely."

"Are you going to murder them?"

"I don't think so."

"But what's more definite than murder?"

"Tax loopholes for the rich."

Peter spoke in a conspiritorial tone. *"You could get one of them with an accidental crossbow discharge. Say it went off while you were cleaning it."*

"And what do I do about the other one?"

"Get him the same way."

"Isn't that sort of coincidental?"

"Not at all. You'll have had your earlier crossbow accident as dramatic proof of your incompetence with the weapon. Another accident was to be expected. Then tell them you've had enough. You won't try to clean the thing ever again. They'll be so busy thanking you for that, they'll forget all about the two corpses."

"Brilliant."

"*Then there's poison. No you've done that. Let's be original. You could lure them both—*"

"Peter."

"*Yeah?*"

"I'm not going to murder anyone." I'd come to the burnt black timber of the village wall. "I'm tired of killings." I reined in and let the two merchants continue on. "I'm tired, I'm tired." I stared at the smoldering wood, the rising threads of smoke, and I smelled the thick odor of char. "This is terrible." My midsection ached. "Christ I'm tired."

"*You want I should pity you?*"

"I can pity me fine by myself." I spat on a beam and it sizzled. "I don't need any help from you."

"*Obviously.*"

"Put on some music."

He gave me a sad piece with violins. "*Music to weep by. Poor Meas. Cry your little eyes out.*"

"You bastard."

"*I beg your pardon. I just happen to have my birth certificate right here in front of me. Not only am I not a bastard, but I'm actually a pedigreed aardvark. Alphabetically speaking, I'm number one.*"

"Soraft," I said despairingly.

"*Yes Gnarla.*"

"Sit on him, would you?"

"*I'm an aardvark,*" Peter said, "*not a chair. Keep away from me. Aardvark aardvark aardvark aardvark aardvark. Gee that's a weird sounding word. But uncle sounds weirder. Uncle uncle uncle uncle uncle.*"

"*He refuses to let me sit on him,*" Soraft said. "*He's running all around the cabin flapping his arms. I think he's gone mad.*"

"*Uncle aardvark uncle aardvark uncle aardvark uncle aardvark uncle aardvark.*"

"*I can't do a thing with him,*" Soraft said.

"He must be stir crazy," I said. "Do you know how to shut off the radio there at your end?"

"*I believe I do.*"

Peter chanted, "*This is Uncle Aardvark's cabin.*"

"Push the button," I said.

Blessed silence descended. Even the sad violin music went off the air, and I was glad I didn't have to listen to it any more. I rode into the ruined village. Utole was doling out his salve to the people with burns. He glanced up and glared at me as I passed, and I got the feeling he considered me to be the evil genie here. Well so did I.

Gangot was with a gaggle of the village elders, nearly all of whom were screaming in rage at him. He was still on his multipede, the elevation giving him, I presumed, a psychological advantage. A group of his men were drawn up behind him, crossbows at the ready, in case his advantage needed enforcing. Other groups of his men were keeping a watch on other groups of villagers. I reined in at his side, and raised my voice above the din.

"Is anyone dead?"

"None of ours," he said loudly.

"Any of theirs?"

He gave the vociferous elders a pained look. "A few of them died in the fire. Most got out in time. And one young boy tried to assault a soldier with a hoe. The soldier shot him through the heart."

"How old was the boy?"

"Very young and headstrong," Gangot said. "The soldier is also young. He acted thoughtlessly and excessively, out of fear and bewilderment. I'd like to order twenty lashes for him, if that meets with your approval."

"Twenty lashes?" I frowned.

Gangot stared at me without expression. "I will not tolerate unnecessary violence by my men. We are neither butchers nor bandits. We are a disciplined army, and we'll behave like one."

"I approve of that," I said. "But henceforth you can order these things on your own. You don't need my approval."

Gangot turned to one of the men behind him. "Take Kylk out and punish him. See that it's done in full view of the soldiers and the villagers alike. Go and do it immediately." The man saluted and rode off, and Gangot turned back to me. "A very bad thing, this whole incident."

I agreed. "Deplorable."

"More than you know," Gangot said. "Kylk has a brother about the same age as the dead boy. For that matter so have I. But Kylk's remorse over the death is great. He's inconsolable. He'll punish himself for a long while after the welts from the whip have healed. I'm afraid I've lost a soldier."

"What are you going to do with him?" I said.

Gangot shrugged. "For now I'll put him with the cooks, away from any kind of a combat situation. He may come around eventually."

"Was this the trouble you wanted to see me about?"

"No." Gangot motioned at the clamoring elders, one of whom took a nervous step backward. "This."

"Oh," I said.

"Do you understand their language?"

"After a fashion."

"Then talk to them," Gangot said. "Quiet them down. Do something with them. Tell them not to worry. We aren't going to harm them. Send them to see the whipping. Send them anywhere. Tell them we're sorry this had to happen. Just quiet them down."

"I'll try." But first I explained to him the relocation plan for the villagers.

When I was finished he said, "How soon would you like to begin preparations to move them?"

"At once," I said.

"Right."

Gangot nodded and wheeled his multipede, and went to notify the troops. The crossbow contingent behind him rode off too, leaving me alone to mollify the village elders. I turned to them with no precise idea of what to say. Then I saw Parell, minus Mexag, coming towards me. He had one of the villagers in tow, a tall stooped man with graying hair. They were both on foot. They stopped beside my multipede, and looked up at me ingratiatingly.

"Is it true kirlu," Parell said, "that the property of these people will not be confiscated?"

"It's true," I said. "They'll be required to pay us a tribute, but most of their property will remain theirs."

"And we will carry on normal trade relations?"

"As far as I know."

Parell indicated the villager. "This is Lupinalta. We've been trading together for many years."

"Greeting," Lupinalta said haltingly. "Parell and me trade much. We trade grain. I trade for all here."

"I speak your language," I told him in his own dialect, and the elders shut up and began to listen attentively.

Lupinalta grinned. "That's marvelous. I can barely get along in yours. Let me see. Where was I?"

"Trading grain," I said.

"I represent my village." His grin was still firmly in place. "Parell here and I have been dealing together long enough to be sure that we can trust each other. He drives a hard bargain though."

"I have to make an honest profit," Parell said mildly.

"But of course you do." Lupinalta's grin was indefatigable. "I meant no offense. Everyone likes to make an honest profit."

"What do you want of me?" I said.

He aimed his grin at my throat. "A judgment from a person who is clearly judicious. We wanted to ask you whether Parell might not be elected your trade representative here."

"Not today," Parell said. "But some day after this turmoil of war has ended. Do you think that might be possible?"

"Perhaps," I said noncommittally.

Lupinalta took my tone to be a dismissal. "Thank you." He bowed to me lavishly and walked away.

I said to Parell, "Since you speak their language, you've found yourself a new job. You may add to your duties as guide those of interpreter."

"As you wish," he said.

I turned to the village elders. "I'll be with you in a moment." I turned back to Parell. "Where's Mexag gotten to lately?"

"He's taking inventory of their stores."

I blinked at him in astonishment. "But weren't they all burned in the fire?"

"On the contrary," he said. "Much of the grain is kept in barns outside the village. None of the barns were damaged."

"That was a stroke of luck." And a small bit of balm for my conscience. "By the way. Lupinalta didn't seem to be very upset by all this. Doesn't he live here?"

"He does live here, and he was upset."

"Was he?"

"Business is business," Parell said, "and a real businessman can conceal his emotions. Lupinalta is a real businessman."

"I thought he grinned too much."

"The alternative was to scowl too much."

"I see what you mean," I said. "Well Commander Gangot could probably use an interpreter just about now. You'd better go and report to him."

"I will." Parell hesitated. "One thing."

"What's that?"

"Forgive my curiosity," he said. "But you say you've never been here before. How is it you speak the language?"

"I have a gift."

"Like being able to read the future?"

"Sort of," I said.

"That must be useful." He continued to hesitate. "I do hope you'll consider making me trade representative."

"The Derone will make the appointment."

"But your recommendation would be important." He smiled at me. "Meanwhile I will do my best as interpreter." He walked away.

"Peter," I subvocalized.

The radio clicked on. "*Yeah?*"

"Are you over your spell of madness?"

"*For the time being.*"

"Good."

"*Are you over your spell of selfpity?*"

"For the time being."

"*Good.*"

I smothered a chuckle and said, "I have an intuition that Parell and Mexag won't be troubling me any more on this trip."

"*I think you're right. Real businessmen don't fuck up their sources of potential revenue. Real businessmen stay cool.*"

"And grin a lot."

"*Instead of scowling.*"

"Absolutely."

"*Another problem solved.*"

"But there's always more to come." I turned to the village elders. "We're sorry this had to happen."

They crowded around me.

Napoleon's disastrous winter retreat through Russia probably had more military flair and martial elegance than our trek across the plains to the next village. Just picture about a thousand mounted fighting men ushering about four hundred ragged and disgruntled peasants, and picture the peasants with their assorted paltry possessions and babies and children and livestock and so forth. Imagine the sound effects. That might give you an inkling, but only an inkling, of what our excursion was like. And don't forget to include the brazier in the sky as the incandescent lighting for the scene.

I'd made a dire mistake letting on that I spoke the language. Seeing that I wore the robes of a holy man and professed compassion, the elders must have concluded that I was the complaint department. I was made as much a victim of their calamity as they were. They marched along beside me steadfastly throughout the entire trek, filling my ears with an endless reprise on the terrible awful inhuman injustice of it all.

Utole rode with us for a while. But he did a quick fade when the elders, doubtless reasoning that a physician must share certain attitudes with a holy man, placed him in the complaint department too. They didn't even seem to care that he was completely unfamiliar with their dialect, so maybe an ignorance of the language wouldn't have saved me from them after all. In a pinch almost any indulgent ear would suffice. Comprehension apparently wasn't one of the requirements.

I asked Utole to stay with me, but he claimed he felt superfluous. There was nothing he could do here that I couldn't manage just fine by myself. He bestowed upon me sincere condolences, and rode off to seek a more taciturn climate. The elders kept on with their woes and lamentations. And long before we came within sight of the next village on our hit list, I was praying in earnest that all of them would suddenly die of old age. Regrettably none of them did.

"Hey Meas, guess what."

"What?"

"The next village knows that you're coming."

I grimaced. "Are you sure?"

"Unless my eyes have begun to deceive me. I can see them getting ready for you. So much for the ever popular element of surprise."

"Have you any idea how they found out about us?"

Peter paused, then said, *"Do you recall those farms outside the last village?"*

"Yeah."

"Well some of the farmers who lived on those farms got away. I saw them ride over here to this village. A few minutes later every man here was up in arms. That intrigued me. I fed the information into the ship's computer. A hypothesis was formulated. The computer and I concur. Them lousy farmers finked on you."

"Why didn't you mention this earlier?"

"Because I thought that you had enough shit on your mind without me burdening you with more."

The next village was distantly visible on the horizon, but I couldn't make out the specific details yet. "A little more shit never hurt anyone, as the politicians prove to us daily. From now on don't try to spare me the burdens."

"*Okay I won't.*" Peter chortled like a heavy in a melodrama who's just been given a mortgage to foreclose. "*I promise.*" He chortled again. "*From now on you get the shit straight.*"

"Terrific," I said.

I bid a fond farewell to the elders, and rode up to the front of the line. Gangot and Utole were waiting for me there. Half a kilometer ahead of us, the village also waited. Apple and pear orchards surrounded it, but I could see no sign of the population. I had a feeling that they could see us though. Gangot gave orders, and we moved out.

The refugees stayed under guard behind us as we advanced. Parell and Mexag remained with them as interpreters, but Utole insisted on riding along with us. He wanted to be near the battlefield in case he was needed.

We approached the village in a slow and stately procession, the troops spread out into formal drill team ranks of fifty. I had a frail hope that the style and size of our force would intimidate the people up ahead enough to make them reconsider their plan to resist us. I thought of the apemen in the forest, and of what had happened to them, and I didn't want to see that happen here. But even before we'd advanced as far as the orchards, I grew certain that my hope had been a very frail one indeed.

I heard somebody shout. And then the men of the village ahead stepped out from in back of their thatchroofed huts, and began to resist us vigorously by shooting arrows and hurling spears and stones. The arrows were falling shy of us by at least seventy or eighty meters, and the spears and stones weren't reaching anywhere near that far. Peter put on some bagpipe music.

"It's time for a policy review," I told Gangot.

He made a peremptory gesture to halt the troops, and the arrows and spears and stones stopped coming. "Well kirlu?"

"We have two choices," I said. "One is that we ride right

in there and crush those people like insects with our unquestionably superior strength. But I don't like that."

He shaded his eyes with a hand, and squinted at the villagers. "We can take them without any inconvenience. There's only about a hundred of them."

I nodded. "And our weapons are also superior to theirs, which makes choice number one a sure thing."

"But you don't like it," Gangot said.

"I dislike the idea of our losing men and material unnecessarily, and of our killing anyone unless killing them is clearly unavoidable."

"Then what's the second choice?"

"To negotiate with them," I said.

Utole spoke from my left. "We ought to try that."

"Our terms," Gangot said, "are unconditional surrender."

My midsection twinged. "I know."

"They seem to be more than prepared to fight us." Gangot indicated the village militia. "Will they agree to a total surrender?"

"I'll go and ask them," I said. "I don't look like a soldier. They shouldn't feel threatened by me."

"I want to go with you," Utole said.

I turned to him. "Why?"

"Because you're still not over your sickness, and I'd hate to see anything happen to you, I mean while you're trying to make peace, and I don't look any more like a soldier than you do, and they might decide to take you hostage, and someone will have to come back here and—"

"All right," I said. "You can come."

Utole and I walked to the village in the hot late morning sunlight. Neither of us made any special remarks or comments to the other. We simply walked along, Utole in his toga, me in my robes, and we didn't say anything. The idea of us going on foot was mine. I figured we'd appear to be less dangerous that way, and the hell with the psychological advantages of being mounted.

We were traveling down an avenue between the groves,

with the apple and pear trees on alternate sides of us. When we came to the arrows shot earlier, sticking out of the ground like quills, we glanced at each other. We were now within range. But there was no reason why the people up ahead should attack a pair of unarmed civilians, one of whom was a holy man and the other of whom was a slender innocuous youth. There was no cause at all for worry. I kept on telling myself that, over and over and over and over.

Finally we got to within hailing distance, and nobody threw any spears or stones, and nobody shot any arrows at us. And nobody hailed us either, but a man moved away from the group. He didn't come out to meet us, he just separated himself from his companions, and he waited for us to get there.

He was a stocky bowlegged man of medium height and age, with broad powerful shoulders and a barrel chest. Across his dark left cheek was a long pink scar from a gash that must have gone most of the way in. The wound had healed improperly, twisting his face into a permanent snarl of rage. He had other scars too.

"Who are you?" he asked when we got to him.

"Gnarla is my name," I said. "And this is Utole. He doesn't speak your language."

Scarface pointed to the massed soldiers behind me. "Why have you come here with that army?"

"I've come to talk," I said. "The army has come to fight. Are you willing to talk?"

"About what?" he said.

"Surrender."

"No," yelled someone in the group.

Someone else yelled, "We fight."

"We fight."

"We fight."

"You'll all be killed," I said.

"We fight."

"We fight."

"Do you want to be killed?" I said. "Is that what you want? Do you want to be killed?"

"We fight."

"We fight."

"We fight."

Scarface balled his fists and took a step towards me. "Haven't we got enough trouble with drought and disease and bad crops and wild beasts and marauders?" He grabbed me by the front of my robes and shook me. "Why have you come here to take what little we have away from us?"

"Please don't do that." His shaking wracked my midsection with agony. "You're hurting me."

"Let go of him." Utole leaped forward and seized the man's wrist. "Can't you see he's ill?"

The words were foreign to Scarface, but he released me anyway. I stumbled and went to my knees, then struggled to my feet again. Scarface jerked away from Utole and glared at me. The villagers had all gone silent, as though they'd abruptly forgotten the script. Utole came over to me.

"How do you feel?" he asked with concern.

"Battered," I said.

Scarface motioned to get my attention. "Go back and tell your army that we will fight and not surrender."

I grimaced. "You'll lose."

"Go and tell them."

"But you haven't a chance."

"Tell them," he said.

"They've already burned the village near the forest to the ground." I gestured towards the refugees, who could be seen beyond the army, silhouetted against the horizon. "The people of that village are there. They want you to help them rebuild their homes. What help can you give them if all of you are dead?"

"We will fight because we must," Scarface said, and the villagers behind him were silent. "We are men and we will fight."

"And die."

"We will die like men."

"You will die," I said, "and you will be buried, and the dirt won't care whether you were men or not. But your wives and your children will care. What will they do after all of you are gone, visit your graves and try to remember how it was to have you with them?"

His scar twitched with the action of his jaw muscles. "I can see why you were the one who was sent to do the talking. You almost make me believe that you yourself actually care about what happens to us."

"I do," I said.

He stared at me, then at the army, then at me again, and he said softly, "What will be done to us if we surrender?"

"Nothing."

"Will we be enslaved?"

"You'll be governed," I said. "There's a difference. New lines of trade will open up for you, and you'll be more prosperous than ever before. You aren't going to lose your property. A tribute will have to be paid, but not an excessive one. In no way will any of you be harmed. I guarantee you that."

"This is the end of our independence." It seemed utterly wrong that a man with a face as proud and furious as his should sound so resigned. "Tell the army to come, we won't fight them."

"But we must fight," someone shouted from the midst of the silent group. "We must fight them."

Scarface picked him out, and went over to him, and said very quietly, "Fight me instead."

"You're not my enemy," said the man.

Scarface gave him a shove. "Am I your enemy now?"

"I don't want to fight you." The man was tense. "I know how strong you are. You could take me easily."

"Not as easily as that army could take us all," Scarface said. "We must not be idiots and refuse to admit defeat."

I turned to Utole. "Let's go."

"Will there be a battle?" he asked.

"Not this time," I said. "They aren't idiots."

We started walking back, and the sun was hot, and my midsection throbbed, and I felt weak, and I felt drained, and I felt worn out, and everything blurred,
        and I fainted.

"Gnarla can you hear me?"

"Unnhh," I said.

"Can you open your eyes?"

"Ooooo." I opened my eyes, and saw Utole. "Rrrrr." I was lying on a straw mattress in a hut. "Aaaaa."

"Can you sit up?"

"I think so." I did so.

He held out an earthen bowl. "Drink this."

"You're always trying to get me to drink something."

"Drink," he said.

"What is it?" I asked suspiciously.

"Just water."

I glanced into the bowl. "What are those tiny things swimming around in there?"

"Bugs," he said.

I drank it down anyway, and it was good, but the bugs I spat out. "How long have I been unconscious?"

"A full day."

"That's too long," I said. "Where's Gangot?"

"He's somewhere in the village."

"Go and get him."

"You ought to rest," Utole said. "At least for another day. You can't keep on like this."

"I've had enough rest already." I drank some more water, and spat out more bugs.

"Gnarla—"

"We aren't going to waste another day," I said. "Another day would be too long. Get Gangot, would you?"

He sighed. "All right." He left.

"*Congratulations Meas on your second village. You did a lot better with this one.*"

"Thanks."

"*And unlike your pal the physician I'm not going to try and convince you to rest on your laurels.*"

"I'm glad."

"*In my opinion sunshine and fresh air and exercise are essential to everyone's health and well being.*"

"I couldn't agree with you more."

"Especially exercise."

"Most assuredly."

"Of course too much exercise can be bad."

"How true."

"But I happen to have inside information that the next village is going to be a pushover."

"Really?"

"A piece of cake."

"Did they hear we were coming and decide that our force is magnificent and altogether invincible?"

"Not exactly."

"What then?"

"I'd rather explain when you get there."

"Why?"

"I don't want to burden you."

"Peter we've been through all that before."

"I still think that I should wait."

"Come on."

"No I'm going to wait."

"Soraft."

"He's asleep. And speaking of Soraft, something's bothering him. I'm not sure what. It might be homesickness. But I have a feeling it's something else. He makes me fidgity, the way he's been acting."

"Maybe you offended him."

"I wouldn't do that."

"Oh no?"

"The argument about things being done the way they're done because that's the way to do them was the last argument we had of any kind."

"Maybe it's your general attitude that offends him."

"But he isn't acting offended, he's just acting strange. He mopes around. He answers me in monosyllables. Most of the time he's into the library, or he's asleep or he's staring at nothing. And he keeps putting off regenerating his new hand. I don't know what to make of him."

"The best thing that you can do is to leave him alone to work it all out for himself."

"*I suppose.*"

"So explain to me."

"*What?*"

"Why the next village is going to be such a pushover."

"*You'll see when you get there.*"

And after that he shut up.

Gangot arrived, and he didn't ask me how I felt, but only said, "The physician says you say you're ready to go."

"Ready and willing and possibly even able," I said. "Have you had any problems with the people here?"

"None."

"How are the refugees doing?"

"Lodging has been secured," he said, "for the infants and the senile and the infirm, and the rest have returned to the village to begin rebuilding."

"Did you send an armed escort back with them?"

"I sent thirty soldiers who, along with a crew of men from this village, will aid in the project."

"Fine," I said.

Gangot gestured. "I sent the soldiers back on foot, and a few of the others will remain here. A use has been found for their clarows. Oh and the leader of this village would like to see you before we go."

"Where is he?"

"Outside," Gangot said.

I got up a bit unsteadily and went through the door of the hut. The sunshine blinded me for a moment, and then I saw Scarface, standing by himself beside an artesian well. Gangot went off to get the troops together. Scarface turned at my approach, his expression indelibly etched with fury. But his voice was still as sombre and resigned as it had been the last time I'd seen him.

"Have you recovered?" he asked.

"More or less."

He fixed his gaze on the well. "I hadn't realized that you were wounded. I would not have treated you so roughly had I known."

"Forget it," I said.

"Some of our young men have joined you." His tone was weary. "They were impetuous and eager to fight, and this is one way they may do so."

I inspected a rock on the ground. "I'm certain they'll be a credit to your village." The phrase sounded trite and inadequate.

"They've been given clarows to ride," Scarface said listlessly, "and splendid new weapons to use. They are anxious to be on their way. I tried to persuade them not to leave, but they wouldn't listen to me."

"Young men are like that," I said.

"Yes."

He examined his well, and I examined my rock, and finally I said, "I've got to go."

"This well has been dry for many years." He kicked lightly at the side of it. "We have another one, not far from here. That one gives us water." He turned from the well, and met my eyes. "Take care of our children. They're all we have."

"Sure," I said.

I walked away through the sunshine, and the last I saw of him he was still standing there by the well, staring down into the darkness.

The day was hot as usual. We rode along to the next village, and the land began to get hilly. I learned that several of the former merchants who were travelling with us spoke the local dialects, and that one of them had been left behind with the soldiers at the last village to do the interpreting. He wasn't anyone that I knew.

Meanwhile Parell and Mexag had spoken with Scarface about them cornering the village's apple and pear market. All they needed to really get things going properly, Parell told me, was for the Derone to appoint them his representatives. He hinted rather blatantly that my support might earn me a partner's share in the profits.

I told him we'd see about that when the campaign was over, and he took my answer to be a conditional affirmative.

Actually his chances were nil. I didn't like him no matter what sort of a pretense he made at being sweet and cordial to me, and I wouldn't have supported him in any appointment except possibly to a garbage detail. There was no sense in telling him that ahead of time though. He would have just gone back to busting my ass again, and I felt I could do quite nicely without the aggravation.

Eventually we came to the next village. Gangot deployed the troops in showy stylish ranks of fifty, and we advanced at a slow processional speed, and then halted about a hundred meters from the nearest hut. A couple of dogs ran out and barked at us. That was the only sign of life, other than some random livestock. The village looked pretty much deserted. Gangot gave orders, and we advanced closer, and more dogs appeared, but that was all.

"Peter explain this," I subvocalized. "There's no one here. Where the hell is everybody?"

"*In a big village by a marsh. It's about ten kilometers away. But you can see what I meant before. This one's a pushover.*"

"Okay now tell me the bad part."

"*You'll see soon enough.*"

"Fuck that shit, tell me now."

"*Do I have to?*"

"Come on come on."

"*This isn't the only village that defected to the big one. More than a dozen others have taken asylum there too.*"

"And I suppose that each and every man of them is anxiously awaiting our arrival and ready to repel all boarders."

"*That's about right.*"

"Jesus."

"*I knew you didn't want to hear about this.*"

"A dozen villages."

"*More than a dozen. I thought that a round figure wouldn't be as menacing. For the initial impact I mean.*"

"How many men do they have?"

"*A lot.*"

"Could you give me a rounder figure?"

"*There's at least a couple of thousand.*"

I grimaced. "Peter."

"*What?*"

"We're not going to talk them out of it this time."

"*I don't think so either.*"

"This time we'll have to fight them."

"*Yeah.*"

I went and told Gangot what was happening, and what we could expect as a probable result. He seemed neither pleased nor displeased by this further evidence of my ability to read the future. He simply gave orders, and the troops went from parade ranks of fifty to travel ranks of five, and we moved out again. We skirted the edge of the empty village, and continued on towards the big one. The barking dogs chased us only so far. They stopped at the line that marked their territorial limit, an invisible boundary X number of meters outside the village.

Dogs have a tremendous sense of territory. For that matter, people have too. The difference is that people don't stop. They just keep on going as far as they can, crossing oceans or space or their fellows, whatever may stand between them and their goal. That's why people are better than dogs, and that's why they're worse. The refusal to put up with limits is the source of man's nobility. And I think if we ever come to that, it will also be the source of man's extinction. *Sic gloria transit, caveat emptor,* and *tempus fugit.* I'm certain the answer to everything must be in one of those somewhere.

And thousands of people were gathered in front of the village. We halted atop a hill a few hundred meters away from them, and for a long sweltering moment nobody moved on either side. In the fields ahead of me corn and wheat bowed and rippled in a gentle breeze. Behind me the troops were drawn up, rank upon rank on their multipedes, waiting for the signal to attack. The marsh that Peter had mentioned wasn't visible from where I was, but I thought I could smell something vaguely swampy in the distance. That might have been my imagination though.

After a while a small group of men detached themselves from the much larger group below and began to walk towards us. Utole and Gangot and Parell and Mexag and I, we watched as they came up the road, with the farmlands all around them, and the sun beating down like a hammer. It was late afternoon. There were only a few more hours of daylight left, but I was sure this thing would be finished one way or the other before night fell.

When the group from the village got close enough, I dismounted and called out to them, "Do you wish to surrender?" and I could hear Parell translating for Gangot and the rest behind me.

The group came closer still, and one of them said, "We have come to ask you to pass us by." He looked very frightened, but his voice was firm.

"We will not pass you by," I said.

"We will not surrender."

"Our forces are strong."

"Our men are many," he said.

"Surrender and save your lives."

"Pass us by and save yourselves."

"No," I said.

"Is that final?"

"Yes."

"Then there is nothing more for us to discuss." He stared at the troops. "Will we be allowed to go back and fight for our land?"

"You can go," I said. "And when you get back we will come. If you change your minds, throw your weapons away. I promise you that no one will be harmed."

"We will not change our minds." He and the others turned, and started down the road again.

Gangot gave orders to his troops. Utole came with me reluctantly when I told him we'd better get out of the way. We rode to another hilltop and watched. It was an awful thing to see. The army was divided up into two approximately equal waves. The first wave spread out in a long single file line across their hilltop with the road to the village as the nexus. These were all trained soldiers on their saddled multipedes. The new recruits were being kept behind with the second wave.

The line became steady. Gangot raised his hand above his head and made a quick sharp gesture. The first wave charged and I finally got to see what a stampede of clarows looked like. The attack wasn't perfectly synchronized. Some of the soldiers went down with their animals long before they reached the village. The worst pileup brought six multipedes together in a rolling wailing sea green tangle of legs and men. Four of the riders were trampled and dead before they knew what had got them. The other men chased up their mounts and rejoined the charge as a sort of a miniature rear guard.

Both ends of the line were moving faster than the center. That made the line an arc. From where Utole and I were stationed it seemed to be closing in like a great deadly circle. The villagers held their position courageously and shot arrows and threw spears and stones that occasionally connected with the soldiers' shields and bounced off. On the soldiers' part not a crossbow was fired. The second wave fanned out in ranks of twenty and just before the first wave reached the villagers they started out. And then the first wave hit.

And if the sky had become a huge bubble of blood at that moment and burst and drowned the world the scene couldn't have been more appalling. I can't tell you how many villagers were ripped to shreds in the next few minutes under the razor claws of the multipedes. I do know for certain though that their resolve wavered and broke at the last instant when they suddenly and fully realized what was going to happen to them. And they turned and they tried with impossible desperation to escape. But the bodies behind them were packed too tightly and there was nowhere they could go. The multipedes rode up their backs and the men were savagely ground under and torn apart as the panicky animals twisted and spun and reared and tried themselves to find an escape. There was nothing but death out there and screaming men and howling mindless beasts.

Then the swords came out. Utole made a despairing noise and he covered his face with his hands. But I couldn't do that myself. I had started this thing and if I was any kind of a man at all I could watch it through to its conclusion. And to say that I was stunned by the enormity of the massacre and horrified by my role in it would be an extreme understatement. But I watched to the end and my guts were wrenched by the sight of the carnage. Peter told me later that he'd gotten sick over it and that Soraft had pounded his stump against a bulkhead when the first wave clashed with the villagers. Of all people a drover like Soraft would know what a rampaging clarow could do to flesh and bone.

It didn't take long after that initial strike. The second wave halted some thirty meters from the periphery of the conflict and in almost perfect safety began to pick off the remaining defenders with crossbow quarrels. And then it was over. We lost about two hundred men and the villagers lost nearly ten times as many. The cornfields and wheatfields were ruined. The village had gone from a battle arena to a graveyard in less than three quarters of an hour. The sun was still as bright as before. But as far as I was concerned night had already fallen.

Parell was among the deceased. He'd joined the attack with the same sort of zeal as he's shown for killing those apemen in the forest. Now he'd paid the price. An arrow sprang like a feathery thorn from his neck, and I didn't shed any tears over the corpse. Gangot had survived with minor abrasions. And Mexag had gotten off without a scratch. He'd wisely hung back and come in with the second wave.

Utole was very busy with casualties for the next few days, and everyone else was busy digging deep trenches for the dead. Then we set out to conquer the remainder of the world. I pictured nothing but endless slaughter ahead, but after that last engagement the rest was easy.

Our fame had travelled, and with it went fear. There was

little in the way of resistance to our advance. There were several small skirmishes, one of which was an ambush, attempted while our forces were split. Peter's warning, my crystal ball, saved us. And that was just about the only real fighting we encountered. Mostly we marched. Peter continued to play music for me, and Soraft continued to act strangely.

And eleven days after the main event had taken place the world was ours. We had less than two thirds of the men we'd started the campaign with, but the army had increased to better than twice its original size. A successful army of conquest doesn't have any problem attracting recruits. Weeding them out, that's the problem.

A triumphant return to Klask'an was the final item on our agenda. The villages were being held, for the most part, on their own recognizance. Gangot sent a large contingent ahead to clear a permanent path through the forest, and the rest of us camped on the edge of it and waited for them to finish. Peter of course made the usual cracks about the unlawfulness of defoliation.

My wounds had pretty much stopped bothering me. The days I'd spent in the saddle had been tiring, but they'd also served to toughen my fibre. At night I slept the dreamless sleep of the exhausted. Utole seemed to be in fairly good spirits now that the campaign was over. And the night before we were set to go through the forest again, I was awakened by the abrupt blare of Peter shouting at me.

"Ummph humph," I said groggily.

"*It's lifted off the moon,*" Peter yelled. "*The Grefstyn ship. It's lifted off the moon.*"

I sat up. "Is it coming your way?"

"*Fucking right it is.*"

"Can you—"

"Please excuse me holy man," someone said from behind me. "Am I interrupting anything?"

I turned and saw Mexag. "I was praying."

"Were you now?" he said in Basic.

"*Who's that?*"

"Mexag." I reached under my robes. "Shit."

The gapjumper made a motion with his left hand, in which a heat gun gleamed dully by the moonlight. "Could this be what you were looking for?"

"I was looking for my headache tablets," I said. "But they aren't in the last place I put them."

Mexag smiled. "Strange how things disappear."

"*What's going on down there?*"

"He has my heat gun."

"To be truthful," Mexag said, "this one isn't yours. This one is mine. Yours is in my saddlebag. You didn't even turn over when I took it away from you. You must be a very sound sleeper."

"A little too sound," I said.

"*You should have murdered him.*"

I grimaced. "Yeah."

"*Meas I have to shut off the radio. Those Grefstyn might get me, much as I dislike the idea. And if they do the noise of the ship blowing up would probably kill you.*"

"I'm willing to take the chance," I said.

"*But I'm not willing to take the responsibility.*"

"Peter don't break contact."

"*I've got to.*" And I heard the click of the *Shoten Zenjin* going off the air.

"He broke contact," I said.

"My associates have done the same thing," Mexag told me, "as a possible measure to save my life."

I stood and faced him. "Gee and I thought they only used their radio to liquidate people."

"That's Catherine you're referring to." He shrugged heavily and his features shifted in the moonlight. "A pity about her. She was beautiful and intelligent. As a matter of fact, she was also my wife."

"Oh," I said.

He shrugged again. "Our marriage was one of convenience, arranged by my government."

"She told me she didn't know whether or not there were any more of you nearby."

"I was patched into that conversation," he said. "It was the worst job of interrogating I've ever heard."

"I'm sorry to have disappointed you."

"Actually I was rather amused." He gestured with the heat gun. "But to answer your question. She didn't know exactly where I was at the time. I could have been nearby or not. She and that moron Ricerick were on the inside and I was on the outside."

I stared at the moons and stars in the sky, waiting for the much brighter light of an explosion. "I was sure that you didn't have any more men in the palace."

Mexag nodded. "I was supposed to have been the one to lead this army to victory."

"A shame that I had to steal your show."

"Quite frankly it was," he said. "Military strategy fascinates me. I wanted to try a few things, a few minor tactical innovations, but we can't always have what we want. Anyway Ricerick was supposed to control the old man, and Catherine was supposed to control Ricerick, and I was supposed to lead the army. And then you arrived in your transparent holy man disguise. Would you mind if I ask you, what is your real name?"

"Belaker Meas," I said. "What's yours?"

"Walter De La Mare." He gave me a small mock curtsy, made comic by his chubbiness. "I was named for the poet."

"I'm afraid I'm not familiar with his work."

"Well to be honest he wasn't all that great, but my mother was very fond of him."

"Mothers," I said.

"Marvelous creatures."

"Mine liked poetry too."

"They all do," he said.

He was too far away to reach and it was too soon to try. I shuffled my feet as a test, and he wagged an admonitory finger at me. I scratched my leg. He took a step backward, and cleared his throat. The heat gun was steady in his hand. For a moment we stared at the heavens. The night was infernally hot, as the nights here tended to be, and the sky was cloudless.

"Won't be long now," I said.

"Shouldn't be."

"What sort of weaponry does your ship carry?"

"The best," he said. "And yours?"

"CROWN cultural missions are required by interplanetary treaty to go unarmed." I wondered what his associates thought of that statement, or whether they were even listening to me up in their ship.

De La Mare tugged pensively at his beard. "I find it exceedingly difficult to believe that CROWN honors that particular treaty any more than we do."

"Believe what you will." I remembered then that the girl had told me a man and a woman were in their ship. "How old is your pilot?"

"Twenty," he said.

"That's pretty old."

"How old is yours?"

"Thirteen," I said.

"That's pretty young."

"Yeah it is."

He blinked at me coyly. "May I ask you a question?"

"Sure," I said.

"Were you able to penetrate my disguise as easily as we penetrated yours?"

"No I thought you were just another fat greasy merchant trying to stick his thumb up anybody's ass he could."

He chuckled with gratification. "Bamboozlement is the only art form that I excel in." He waved the heat gun at me. "But you were immediately recognizable for what you are."

I nodded. "My circumcision gave me away."

"That and your attitude," he said. "It really wasn't very professional of you to be so obvious."

"I guess good help is hard to find these days," I said. "And speaking of which, where did Parell come from?"

"He was just a native." The heat gun was aimed directly at me. "He wasn't a bad sort once you got to know him. Of course he was a bit opportunistic."

"Unlike yourself."

De La Mare smiled. "Do I detect a subtle undercurrent of animosity in your tone?"

"Don't be—"

"Look." He pointed upward. "There."

A new sun flared in the sky with an intensely vivid light that banished the stars, a light so brilliant the darkness all around us was totally obliterated. And a moment later the booming roar of the concussion slammed against us. Our ears rang and our eyes were dazzled, and I could have taken him then, but I forgot to make my move.

The entire camp was rattled. The soldiers were jolted rudely from their sleep, and began to dash about in a shrieking superstitious frenzy. But before they could build up much solid momentum at that, they had to stop and calm down their multipedes, since the animals were better at being frenzied than anyone.

"Nice explosion," said De La Mare.

"Ummmm," I said.

And we waited.

"*Hey Meas.*"

"Peter."

"*What's happening?*"

"You beat them." I laughed out loud. "You beat them." I danced a few steps. "You beat them."

"*I certainly did.*"

"That's fucking fantastic."

"*So how are things going at your end?*"

"Hang on."

I checked De La Mare. Under his preposterous beard, his face was tightly set. He glanced down at the heat gun in his hand, and then at the Grefstyn ship blazing in the sky. I tensed to make a lunge while his attention was elsewhere. But before I could move, his gaze had returned to me.

His expression was baleful. "You might as well take this." He tossed me the heat gun.

I caught it and put it away. "Thanks."

"*Is everything okay with you?*"

"Everything's dandy," I said.

Most of the multipedes had been calmed by then. And the soldiers had also quieted down somewhat, and were staring at the conflagration in the sky. The sight was an eerie one, a radiant aureola of fire, with crimson flames at the core, and a bright yellow nimbus. These colors were lovely and pure.

The fire was pulsing rather than flickering, and was surrounded by absolute darkness. I watched for a while, and I tried to imagine what a world would be like where the sky was always black, even during the day. And I decided that life there would no doubt continue in spite of such a sad perversity.

"Where are you going from here?" De La Mare asked me.

"Earth probably."

"I'd like to go with you," he said. "My government won't be happy to see me after this failure, not that I have any apparent way of getting back to them. And CROWN can acquire quite a lot of useful information by debriefing me."

"I thought you hardened professionals committed suicide before you revealed anything to the enemy."

"Nonsense," he said. "There wouldn't be any of us left if we did that. Amateurs commit suicide. A professional is someone who survives."

"Peter," I said.

"*Yeah?*"

"Do you think we should take him with us?"

"*I'll include a request for clarification of his status in the report on this shindig that I'll be sending back to CROWN as soon as I get around to it.*"

"He'll find out for you," I told De La Mare. "So Peter, come on. What was the fight like?"

"*Oh just your ordinary average run of the mill space battle. The guy who was piloting that shit bucket never even got close to me. His reaction time must have been at least two to three tenths of a second off the mark.*"

"He was twenty years old."

"*Well they should have retired him when his reflexes went stale. The fight was nothing. I flew the ship with my usual*" *flair, and the computer manned the ordnance. It wasn't really very exciting. In fact Soraft slept through the whole thing.*"

"That's Soraft for you," I said.

There isn't much more.

Peter sent his report off to CROWN and got back a reply. The reply read, *"Cease all present operations. Retrieve Atherton and Grefstyn agent. Leave natives in charge for the interim."*

We were tramping through the partially defoliated forest when I broached the subject to Utole.

"You mean that you want to make me the next Derone?" he said in utter astonishment.

"It'll give you something to do with your time," I told him. "You can try inventing your own answers to your questions. Think about it."

"I will," he said.

"But will he accept?" Peter asked.

"We'll see," I said.

When we got to the palace, I spoke to Utole again.

"Yes," he said.

"Commander Gangot would make a fine military governor of the provinces," I said. "His entire career has been one long preparation for the job."

"Perhaps," Utole said.

I promoted an audience with the Derone.

"It's time to go," I said.

"I've decided to stay here." Atherton caressed an exquisite

courtesan's naked ebony flank and swigged wine from a filigreed goblet. "These goddam people need me."

I glanced from him to the girl and back. "Are you aware that the incidence of syphilis here is so high that it strikes between sixty and seventy percent of the population?"

He stopped caressing the girl, and stared at me nervously. "No I wasn't aware of that."

"The statistic," I said, "is in a preliminary field survey on this planet which happens to bear your personal signature."

He took a swig of wine. "My signature?"

"That's right."

"I'll be goddamned." He shuddered and took another swig of wine. "Syphilis is horrible."

"So how are you fixed for penicillin?" I said.

He decided on further reflection that maybe he ought to come back with us after all.

"Talk to Soraft, would you?"

"About what?" I said.

"We're going to be leaving in a very short while, and the tissue is ready for regeneration, and he still won't take the new hand."

"Did you ask him why?"

"I thought you should be the one to—"

"There is no way," Soraft cut in, *"that I could explain the new hand when I return to my friends. And Gnarla I must return to them. They would not understand such a miracle, just as I myself do not understand it. But they would be frightened, and I could not explain. This is why I have got to refuse the new hand."*

"I see," I said.

"And there are so many other things I must try to explain to them. That our way should truly be examined. That our goals may indeed be false ones, born of a senseless observance of pointless custom. That there should be more to our lives than travelling from one barren place to another, trying to earn enough to go on travelling from one barren place to another."

I frowned. "Will they listen to you?"

"*They will probably kill me,*" he said quietly. "*But I will try to explain to them anyway.*"

"I wish you luck," I said.

That night another star fell from the Jsimaj sky, not far from the outskirts of Klask'an. It disgorged one passenger in exchange for three more. That passenger met me at the bottom of the access ramp. I gripped his wrists for a moment, and his one hand gripped me back. Then he mounted one of the multipedes we had ridden across the desert.

"What should I do with these others?" he said.

"Throw away their saddles," I told him, "and take them with you. Say you've been out searching for strays."

"I'll say they were a gift from the kirlu who fought with us against the bandits."

"At least somebody on this planet will remember me kindly," I said, more bitterly than I'd intended.

He gave me a long level look. "Has your visit here really accomplished anything of value?"

I scuffed my foot in the sand. "I don't know."

"Will you ever return?"

"Not me," I said. "But someone will. Just keep your head up. Watch for falling stars."

"I'll do that."

"Goodbye Soraft."

"Goodbye kirlu," he said.

He waited there while we climbed the ramp to the cool illuminated spaceship cabin. Then he rode off, into the darkness. Peter met us at the airlock, red hair and freckles and all. He still had the same sweet and charming demeanor that had endeared him to me from the start. He indicated De La Mare and Atherton, both of whom were bearded and fat.

"Which of these slobs is which?" he said.

I introduced them. "And this is Mr. Donovan our pilot."

"Hello." De La Mare bowed to him.

Atherton swayed drunkenly back and forth. "Goddam." He'd thrown himself one hell of a going away party just before we left.

"I should have recognized his breath," Peter said to me. "You always make my ship too crowded."

"You always complain." I paused. "But much as I hate to admit it I'm glad to see you again."

"You'll get over it eventually," he said. "And much as I hate to admit it myself—"

I nodded. "Yeah."

"Well come on everyone," he said briskly. "Get aboard. We're on a tight schedule here. Can't let the natives see us. That's strictly against the rules, as I'm sure we all know. Get aboard."

We got aboard.

About the Author

Bob Toomey was born, appropriately enough, on Labor Day in 1945. He was educated in Roman Catholic schools in Massachusetts by the Sisters of St. Joseph. For a nickel he will shyly exhibit the scars he received during that period. Upon graduation from high school he immediately joined the United States Navy, and almost as immediately the United States Navy discharged him, the cause being an inability to adjust to military service. He continued to display this inability to adjust in civilian life as well. He went through the usual number of trial careers, including turret lathe machinist, civil engineer, investigative reporter, and master criminal, before he finally resorted to fiction writing. By then he knew that he would never be respectable anyway. His former wife agrees with this, and recently their divorce became final. Politically he considers himself to be about medium left. He honestly believes that everyone should be allowed their freedom so long as he isn't required to make a cash contribution to it. His hobbies are film and literary criticism, music, travel, and trying to quit smoking. *A World of Trouble* is approximately his first novel.

SELECTIONS FROM THE PUBLISHER
OF THE BEST SCIENCE FICTION
IN THE WORLD

———◆———

SPRING 1973

To order by mail, send $1.25 per book plus 10¢
for handling to Dept. CS, Ballantine Books,
36 West 20th Street, New York, N. Y. 10003

1972 SELECTIONS FROM
THE PUBLISHER OF THE BEST
SCIENCE FICTION IN THE WORLD

The World's Best
Adult Fantasy
Ballantine Books
Spring — 1973

The World's Best Adult Fantasy
Ballantine Books
1972

THE WORLD'S DESIRE
H. Rider Haggard and
Andrew Lang

XICCARPH
Clark Ashton Smith

THE LOST CONTINENT
C. J. Cutliffe Hyne

DOMNEI
James Branch Cabell

DISCOVERIES IN
FANTASY
Edited by Lin Carter

KAI LUNG'S GOLDEN
HOURS
Ernest Bramah

DERYNI CHECKMATE
Katherine Kurtz

BEYOND THE FIELDS
WE KNOW
Lord Dunsany

THE THREE
IMPOSTORS
Arthur Machen

THE NIGHT LAND,
Volume I
William Hope Hodgson

THE NIGHT LAND,
Volume II
William Hope Hodgson

THE SONG OF
RHIANNON
Evangeline Walton

GREAT SHORT NOVELS
OF ADULT FANTASY 1
Edited by Lin Carter

EVENOR
George MacDonald

To order by mail, send $1.25 per book plus
10¢ for handling to Dept. CS, Ballantine Books,
36 West 20th Street, New York, N.Y. 10003.